Six Women 6 Flavors

FROM YOUR HEAD TO YOUR BED

erotic fiction

A.D. WHITE

 Indie Owl Press

Indie Owl Press

818 SW 3rd Ave #221-2455
Portland, OR 97204-2405

info@indieowlpress.com
IndieOwlPress.com

Six Women 6 Flavors

www.DavidWhiteAuthor.com

First U.S. Edition, 2017

ISBN-10: 0-9990126-2-2
ISBN-13: 978-0-9990126-2-8
LCCN: 2017955503

Printed in the U.S.A.

Dedicated to Thinkers with a Sexual Appetite

"For women, the best aphrodisiacs are words.
The G-spot is in the ears.
He who looks for it below there is wasting his time."
— Isabel Allende

CONTENTS

INTRODUCTION

What is this five-foot-eight-inch guy with a 40-inch waistline doing with that attractive girl who looks like Beyoncé Aniston, or Halle Johannsson? He must have a huge wallet? No, I bet she lost a bet or her eyesight. Maybe, he just makes her laugh, or he just says what she needs to hear. In my 33 short years of life, I have had a few women out of my league, maybe one or two, but in most cases, we were equally matched at the time of dating. What I have noticed is that physical attraction and security are essential to most women but not as important as confidence and mental stimulation.

I want to take my readers on a journey through some of my experiences ranging from intellectual connections to sexual encounters. No, I am not a sex guru, nor am I a guy who has knocked it out of the ballpark every time. When going out with friends, there were times I got the best girl out of the group, and times where I had to take one for the team. I would never claim to look like a young Denzel or Pitt or to have the physique of an Olympic track athlete. I consider myself average in many ways, but advanced in my sense of self and humor. I am confident, but more so competitive, always aiming to win, regardless of the opponent.

I appreciate the female perspective and their delicacy. I think a corporate team is incomplete if a female is not included. When it comes to uniting a man and a woman, it is possible that they can fall in pure innocent love at first sight. However, there are times when strategy and negotiations are required to make a long-term connection. In this book, I will discuss both, but mostly the latter. I have a bit of an old-fashioned mentality in perceiving men as the hunters who should go after what they want. I do not oppose women approaching men, but just like women who do not like men who are too aggressive, I prefer women who aren't too forward, especially in our society where men are conditioned to avoid women who seem desperate. When the connection is right, one party having to win the others heart or attention is my kind of game.

I have had some exciting encounters with different types of women. Great physical features can always get the blood flowing to the right regions of the body. Some people have sexual partners because it is convenient. A common excuse is, we are neighbors, and if someone is lonely or needs to release some sexual tension, we support each other. We all know someone who has a sexual partner because there is no hassle attached to it or commitment other than safe sex. Even sex with your spouse can become banal because the mental stimulation or emotional reactions are either not present or desensitized. Sometimes sex with someone who you are less familiar with encourages you to be more impressive and pleasurable in the bedroom. Sexual encounters happen for many reasons, but the best is often when we share a meeting of the minds with an equally present partner.

When a person's mind is stimulated by someone unexpectedly, they can get curious and want to reveal guarded layers of themselves. This is why some individuals who are in a committed relationship do not even want their mind entertained because that can give access to more, sometimes unconsciously. If I like what a person is saying and how it is said, I may be tempted to want to hear more. Then the exchange of contact information begins and I am delighted when I find someone who is thinking on the same plane as me. Curiosity can be our worst enemy, though. Hearing is the doorway to imagination, and in most cases, it is best not to even engage with the sales pitch.

Humor can also sway attraction. It takes intellect to make your partner laugh because you have figured out what this person interprets or connects to as humorous. When I was 18 or 19 years old—just after moving to San Diego—I went out with a new girl for the first time in this new city. Her name was Amber, and she told me that she was a Jehovah's Witness. During lunch, I made a joke about how it sucks that she probably did not know how old she was because her family never celebrated her birthday. Amber did not find that joke funny at all, and I went from laughing at the joke to regretting that I had ever made a sound. That was Amber's and my first, and last, date. I was not able to recover, and she was closed off mentally for the rest of the day.

The bad experience with Amber was short, but the lesson it taught me was long lasting. First, always be sensitive to the things that make up a person's core values, such as faith and family. Just because she jokes about her dad being absent does not make it okay for me to. Lastly, know your audience before setting up a joke. If you're prone to joke about sensitive topics, it is especially important to make sure that you're with someone who has a light-hearted sense of humor. Some people are like coach Belichick from the New England Patriots or Popovich from the San Antonio Spurs and only laugh twice a year. Humor is a way to someone's heart, but intellect is the path to the bed. My goal is not to guide you in the pursuit of sex, per se; it is in exploring all ways and options for developing a connection that both individuals deem comfortable.

When I decide to make a sexual connection, it is important to me that all of my senses be engage. I need to like what I see from her hips to the lips and more. I like to get familiar with the scent of another person lying next to me. I do not have the best sense of smell, never have, so when I *can* smell, it is keen to the way my body reacts. I like to touch smoothness and firmness. If I caught you off guard and you have a little stubble of hair on your legs, that is okay because perfection is not reality. Rubbing a woman's back and being able to feel their vertebrae and spine while massaging is my preference. I do like a woman with a toned body. However, I do not discriminate against heavier women because a lady's size has nothing to do with her delicacy and value, but I personally prefer an athletic physique. Hearing a woman's reaction to my touch makes me more eager and likely to do more and want more. I recommend that everyone pursue the type of body that they find most arousing as well.

Being a musician, and having an ear and love for tones, vibrations, and pitches have had tremendous impact on me as well. Out of all of my senses, hearing is vital to my sexual appetite. I get most aroused by the sound of sex—the noises of a woman. Depending on the mood, the tone can be quiet and close, vibrating off my neck, or high and erratic, bouncing off the walls of the room. In the midst of sexual intercourse, it can feel good—wet as Niagara Falls, and look as appealing as the moonlight over the ocean. Meanwhile, the movement is equivalent to a ten-thousand-dollar massage chair. It is not until I hear the moan, listen to the commands shouted out, and hear the magic words, "I'm Cumming" in a pleased pitch that I am sexually gratified and able to climax.

Needless to say, negative sounds implore a negative experience. Taste, of course, is also important—no one wants to kiss or lick someone who tastes unclean or tart. Reasonable freshness should always be an expectation in a situation that can lead to sex. After all of the senses are activated, the sixth bonus sense is the psychological reason that ties into emotional. It's more fun sharing unique sexual moments with someone you admire on a cerebral level.

Six Women 6 Flavors

FROM YOUR HEAD TO YOUR BED

-I-

Am I lucky or Cursed

When I was a sophomore in high school, a girl named Carrie told me that she liked me and that I better be her boyfriend or I may have problems with her older brothers. I found that to be humorous, and a little strange. First, Carrie was not a big girl that was intimidating. She was actually quite small, and looked like Jada Pinkett in the early 90's. Secondly, I had older brothers to protect my own interest in safety, so I took her light threat as a joke. What I did not know was that this cute, petite girl was very demanding. Carrie wanted me to meet her after each class period and walk her to class, then wait with her after school until her ride came to pick her up. There was a time her transportation was not able to make it and she told me that my dad needed to give her a ride home. As a 15-year-old kid in the 90's, I did not recognize a control freak. Carrie became a burden more than a blessing and I needed a way out.

Designing an exit strategy was not hard. I thought I was going to have to cheat or get another guy that was better looking than me to take her off my hands. Turned out, all I had to do was become less accessible and move slow to her commands, then let her call it off. For some reason as a youth I never wanted to break up with a girl; I ALWAYS sabotaged my relationships. I preferred for the girl to break-up with me or think I was just not that into them. Having a weak backbone was not my only problem.

In middle school, before Carrie, I had been suckered into being the boyfriend to a girl named Rina. It's not uncommon in middle school during the first two weeks of school for everyone to be wearing their best outfits and fresh hairstyles. It is best to survey the whole 8th-grade class before committing to being with one partner. Apparently, after doing her assessments, Rina decided I was the one. Needless to say, Rina sent a message to me saying she wanted to be my girlfriend, and I felt pressured to say yes, so I did.

I have to admit; 8th grade was when I really started to get into girls. Prior to that, my focus was sports, music, and friends. I was a little naïve; my Dad has only been with my mom, and he was not hip to the tactics of getting girls. My older brothers didn't share their secrets or just weren't around, so I had to fake it until I made it.

Back in the 90's, the most we did in 8th grade was kiss and some heavy touching. Sex was for high school kids or beyond; we knew and honored that rule. Rina and I begin talking on the phone, and she was cool and probably my first real kiss with the tongue. Rina was a light-skinned black girl (maybe Caribbean island background); she had hazel eyes, and wore a freeze style hair during the first two weeks of school.

In week three of our relationship, Rina's eye color changed from hazel green to dark brown, and her hairdo went from a nice big freeze to a little knot of a pigtail. (I think it needs more slack to be considered a ponytail, but it was at least more than a rat's tail.)

This was my first realization that Rina had been presenting a fake persona for the first two weeks of school. I was shocked and slightly reluctant to hold hands with her on that first Monday morning with her unaltered look. Yes, very superficial of me, but I was only 13-years-old. I also had to prepare for the worst because kids back then were cruel, and we weren't fortunate enough to have anti-bully advertisements or support groups. It was easy to go with the crowd, but at least we didn't have cyber bullying and social media humiliation. Rina, at the time, had an older brother going through cancer treatment, and when Rina came to school with the change in hair length, looking far less glamorous, a rumor spread that she had leukemia. Like I said, I was 13, and I was familiar with the term leukemia because three years earlier in 1992 my grandmother had leukemia and she had lost her hair and teeth.

No way in the world was I going to be with anyone who might experience that, so I told Rina over the phone that I did not want to be her boyfriend and withheld the reasons. Yes, I know, I was a young, naïve, little jerk. Fast forward 20 years, I would never breakup with someone I cared about over an uncontrollable change in their health or a vicious rumor.

I broke up with Rina over a rumor, but it was refreshing to randomly run into Rina in 2009, 15 years after middle school. It was good to see how she'd grown into becoming a beautiful, loving mother, and of course cancer free (because she never had it).

Some of my character traits have placed me in positions to feel lucky or cursed. I felt lucky at age 16 when a lady from church asked me to give her daughter Janina piano lessons. I went to her house for the first lesson and discovered that Janina was the prettiest girl I had ever seen in person. Meeting the women in Janina's family was when I found out that Trinidad in the Caribbean nation produces some of the best-looking women in the world. She was only six months younger than me and was a professional teen model. My best friend James and I just referred to her as "the model." We both couldn't believe that I was getting paid fifteen dollars a lesson to hang out with this beautiful girl. It probably took me about four lessons to start hanging out with Janina socially. She was beautiful, smart, and kind-hearted.

Janina and I hung out from time to time, kissed, and did some other things, but I felt I did not have her full attention—possibly because I may not have possessed the necessary confidence or bite to hold onto a girl like Janina. My relationship with Janina was a very pivotal life lesson compounded with personal, relational, and educational tools to bank away for later life encounters. I held Janina in high regards during our on and off again interactions from 16 to 18 years old. In my regular school and neighborhood setting I was confident, a young leader, and I did not find a woman's beauty intimidating. With Janina, it was more than beauty; even as a teenager, she already had a steady stream of high income. She was intelligent, had a plan, and a sexy exotic look, but was still innocent. All of those things faded my confidence. I was still funny and cool to be around, but slow in romantically connecting.

I am a firm believer that nice guys tend to finish last, and girls generally want a guy who has a little bite to him. If a man is too scared to take the girl by her hand and lead her down the romantic path, the guy is setting the stage to be a prime candidate for the friend zone. Janina taught me to have unwavering confidence, even when the girl appears to be out of your league. My early encounter with Janina showed that one does not have to possess perfect physical features to get the attention of an attractive woman, as long as you play to your strengths. Fast forward to present day, Janina turned out to be what I thought she would be. She is beautiful, successful, and smart, with a heart to help others. We even still check-in on each other from time to time.

As a young man nearing adulthood, you have to make a choice about whether you are going to be the guy who is always in a relationship or the person who keeps their options open. At an early age, I was accused by my friend Lawrence of taking too long to close the deal with girls. Lawrence said that I am too nice, and I spend too much time trying to convince new girls I meet that I am genuinely a friend. In social settings, closing the deal is getting the CORRECT contact information to follow-up at a later time. When going to a lounge, bar, or social event, the goal for most men is to play the odds. The more numbers you obtain, the better your chances are of landing a date at another time.

Nevertheless, I have always believed in quality over quantity, and I can tell after having a lengthy conversation with someone if a follow-up phone call is even worth the time. Plus, as a young man, I was still scared to turn down a girl because I didn't want to have to manage rejecting her and her reaction. It is strange how a person can feel guilty or wrong for rejecting someone's interest in them. Walking out of a department store, we're often approached by children asking us to donate to various causes by purchasing candy, often so they can attend some sort of class trip. Even if you do not want the candy, because of their presentation, one may still donate to help their cause. I often do. And I can also get suckered into that same type of sympathy, resulting in giving my number out to a girl whose candy or flavor does not appeal to me. Thereafter, I have to pull out one of my sabotage tactics. Although, every conversation with the opposite sex to me was/is worth something of value because as a man you need to know what a girl wants and how to anticipate those needs.

I have always been a fan of conversation, and fascinated by the mind games between men and women when they first meet. There has to be motives involved, and eventually a plan for the new friendship. Do I want to have sex with this person? Do I want to use this person for their notoriety or affluence? Where do I see things going between us? Is this someone I can mold into being in my support corner? (These are among many possible questions.) Playing the cat and mouse game became fun for me because I felt I was just gaining more experience by living in a female's head. I know people hate when it is called a game, but our society still puts men and women on opposing

6

teams, so that's exactly what it is: a game. And the goal is to go from being two individuals to one united team. After spending so long genuinely trying to understand women—an honest desire—I ended up feeling CURSED because I was becoming more concerned with the female mind than the body.

As a teenager, DJ Quik influenced me through a line in one of his songs that said to get power, money, and then the pussy—in that order. And if you don't you're dumb. These lines put a little more bite in me, and helped to give me a balanced perspective when engaging with women. The word power can be interpreted and achieved by different roads. I did not and do not want the kind of power that prevents my woman from speaking or objecting to my thoughts or ideas. Power that causes intimidation or harm is not healthy to inflict on someone you call a partner. I am not interested in ruling over every decision or personal choice in a relationship. The power that I desire and what I think Quik was referring to is the power of being essential to my woman. The power of becoming part of the girl I am chasing, and essential in her everyday routine. It is not good to be in a situation where a girl or your significant other can go a full 24-hours without missing you after they have not heard from you. After 24-hours my girl should feel that she needs to include me in order to feel fulfilled.

I want the power that expects me to bring laughter, excitement, joy, and ultimately a smile to my girl's day. The power of being a necessity makes me a fore thought in my lady's life. If a woman just views me as a sex toy or a side dish, and counts me out as being a negotiable commodity on a typical day, there is no specialness or absolute in only being physically connected. However, as a man, we have been stereotyped to only care about the goodies, the money, and the heart/romance later, in this specific order. Standing in on a conversation with a bunch of college boys, the question between guys concerning a new girl or relationship is often "Hey, did you smash? Did you hit? Did you get inside?" The question from a male is NEVER, "Hey bro, did you win over her heart?" We all know most male and female desires are different, that is one of the reasons why they say we are from separate planets. But when considering the "long game," are we really *that* different?

Being a competitor, it is very critical to understanding the opposition. Champion athletes like Kobe Bryant, Peyton Manning, LeBron James, Tom Brady, and Serena Williams know how to dominate their opponents. As much as each of them is physically gifted and vigorous, they are also more mentally prepared for what is ahead. Something Kobe and Jordan have said in interviews, that I apply to the women I have dated, is to "know the opponents' tendencies." In basketball, they are saying to know what hand the person you are guarding likes to dribble with when they drive to the basket. What are the pivot moves in the paint? And does smack-talking make the opponent perform better or worse? The same thing goes for dating and advancing in a relationship or conversation.

Author Gary Chapman wrote a book about love languages that addresses our ability to sense or "read" what a person wants or needs because it often manifests as a unique love language. When meeting a girl for the first time or while on a first date with someone there is only a small possibility that you will pick up on the person's love language. Nevertheless, there are standard approaches and things all people want, which I have learned through trial and experience, and it is quite simple. If I am meeting someone for the first time, my primary goal is to get their attention. Obtaining a person's attention can be difficult depending on the setting and under what circumstances our paths cross. People have natural tendencies to use their phone as a barrier or protector when engaging in conversations with a stranger.

For example, if I met someone today, my biggest obstacle would be getting the person to pay attention to me more than their phone. Guys and girls like to use their mobile devices as an excuse, and we have been doing this before cell phones were accessible. Back in the 80's and 90's girls would have a friend call them on a restaurant phone to get them out of a dreadful date. Men pulled similar stunts. We all acted like we were ER doctors, rushing away from the table to handle a phone-call worthy "emergency." Now we think we are slick when we text our friend, asking them to call to get us out of the bind. Sometimes, though, the opposite happens, and you make such a strong connection with someone that you could care less about your phone and hope they feel the same. So how do you master capturing a person attentions right away? Do people still use pickup lines? Some sports teams have better success speeding up the pace of the game, and there are some who strategize to slow it down because of the likelihood of fewer mistakes so they can run their play. Whichever you prefer, stay true to yourself and play *your* game.

Sometimes you have only two minutes to close the deal, sometimes 20 minutes, and sometimes two hours. If you have two minutes, the girl must find you physically attractive and maybe even humorous. Two minutes is not enough time to make a strong connection, but you can make an impression. A good impression can get you a first date, and a connection can buy more time for exploration. If I only have two minutes, I try to show that I am respectful, and a date with me will be fun and entertaining. As we progress in this text, you will see how things formed between each girl and the ways in which every situation, and each girl, was unique. In a post-sports-game conference, the broadcaster may ask Aaron Rodgers, "How were you able to throw three consecutive touchdowns in the final quarter?" A typical answer is, "I just took what the defense gave me." A comment like that means I did not do anything special; the opponent showed their hand and I reacted. A scenario like this happens all the time in the dating world.

When I was 18-years-old, it was my first year in San Diego, California, and I got a job working at an elementary school as the class assistant. During recess, I would go outside and do sports activities with the kids, and everyone wanted to play whatever game I chose for the day. I noticed there was a young, 22-year-old teacher named Christina who was admiring my interaction with the kids. This went on for a week and I took notice of Christina enjoying the fun I was having. Perfect, I had Christina's attention, and it was time to capitalize. One recess I ended the games earlier, so I could make a greater impression on Christina.

"Hey," I said. "I've noticed you watching the games— why don't you join us, and maybe I'll even let your team win a game?"

"Sorry, I'm a teacher, and I can't afford to break into a nasty sweat, I have to go back in to teach my class," she replied.

"Oh, I totally understand. So, what's your name, and what grade do you teach?"

"It's Christina, and I teach the third grade."

"Much respect to you. Teaching children is not an easy task, and it requires a lot of your time lesson planning and sometimes using your own resources. Well, I see you like to watch people have fun. Maybe you can find some time for us to have a playdate when you're not worried about returning to class sweaty?"

She smiled. "Sure, take down my number. And what's your name?

Christina and I talked on the phone for a week before she invited me over to her house to watch a ShowTime television series that we were both following. It was nice to hang out without having to do the fancy date thing and just be in relaxed clothing. The risky thing about us watching TV for the night, though, was that the series did not start until 10 p.m. Fortunately, when I arrived at Christina's house I was pleased with what I saw and smelled. Honestly, some women live like professional wrestlers with laundry all over the place and dishes in the sink.

Christina was an independent young girl, and had a very healthy body with naturally full breasts. Her house smelled like a warm candle was burning with a fresh, spicy citrus fragrance. I could tell after a moment of being in her home that she was into either the African or Caribbean culture. As we sat cozily on her couch we enjoyed the TV show, but also took full advantage of the time to spark some real romance. She invited me to her room in the back, and we started to kiss in her bed; I could not resist caressing her breasts, which offered more than a handful. All of the kissing and touching was getting to be too much for her, and she pulled her underwear down and said, "I want to feel all of you." My blood rushed from my penis to my head, and I didn't want to lunge for her goodies. She was ready to give me her body, but I wanted her mind first.

Men and women occasionally tussle for the upper hand in the relationship. Guys often get controlled when their mate exceeds their physical needs beyond expectation. BabyFace wrote a song in 1990 called "Whip Appeal," essentially saying that when a woman uses her body to mesmerize a man, she puts a whip appeal on her lover, and gains the upper hand. No, I am not saying relationships are all about gaining the upper hand. Everyone can be equal; however, that is rare and not the most common situation. Those who think so are often lying or limited in their experience. Even in "equal" partnerships, the couple is simply taking turns at who has the upper hand at any given moment. Couples that trade off with a pleasing balance tend to last longer.

Christina wasn't necessarily playing any games or approaching our evening with a strategic plan. It is often me who over-thinks the relationship and the romance. It is me who makes me feel cursed because I am always looking to have an advantage when a connection is forming. Maybe it is an insecurity of mine. Either way, at the time, I was convinced I did not want to be the guy viewed as just trying to increase his count of sexual partners. I preferred to be considered warm, intelligent, attentive, and entertaining, because these are the things that I knew would make me become a priority in someone's life.

Young adults have sex with people all of the time, and it doesn't mean much. I have had sex with girls who didn't mean more to me than sex, but it did not give me the connection I desired. I did not have sex with Christina that night and interrupted our physical connection. It is okay for a girl to stop a guy during a moment of physical intimacy, and the same goes for men. Unfortunately, when the roles are reversed it is often viewed by the female that she is being rejected and the male is disinterested. I was interested in Christina, and she was my preferred body type, but my mind affected my body; ultimately, ruining my relationship with Christina before it could fully launch.

-II-

Welcome to the Big Leagues

It is amusing when I hear young adults talk about sex and how they're good in the bedroom. When approached correctly, sex is a selfless act. Sure, most women want to be intimate, and most men want to screw, but there will be a time and place for both. When you are 18 to 21 years old, and perhaps do not have a place of your own, sex becomes challenging, but it can also be thrilling because of the adventure in sneaking around. Also, sex is often still new for someone under 20-years-old. I did start having sex at an early age in high school, but not very frequently. I honestly only needed three to four minutes to finish the job. Young girls try to put out in an attempt to keep the guy's attention or because they do love their mate, but does a 20-year girl know her body? I thought I was a stud in bed at age 20. By that time, I had already participated in the loss of three different girls' virginity and turned down three more. Sex for me did feel good but I wondered how many people were just doing it so that they did not feel left out.

There are other ways besides experience to get better at sex. Sure, the more you shoot a gun, the better you should get at hitting your target. However, people who attend training and learn how to assemble a gun, and who have read literature on different types of guns are better with guns overall. We can all appreciate a good marksman, but I am more impressed with a person who knows their craft and knows gun care. Notice in military training, they do not only teach how to shoot, but they teach you how to become one with your weapon.

The human body is full of sensation, emotion, and pleasure points. It's best to present sex as an art activity, not just for seven minutes of ecstasy. The perineum is the spot of skin between the genitals and the rectum; with the right vibration, and touching of the finger or tongue, it can be stimulating for your partner. Sucking the male testicles while gently stroking the base of his penis or turning the tip of his penis like a doorknob in a firm caressing manner, will increase the erotic moment. There is a G-spot for the man like there is for women, but the human body needs to be studied then explored to find its exact location on each individual. The average person is okay when we are just talking about penetration. But to become an excellent marksman, knowing the weapon inside and out is essential and ultimately rewarding.

Becoming a good sex partner means you have to become a student, per se, in learning how to navigate different sizes and shapes. Men are often too proud to ask for advice or seek book knowledge; we do not like reading instruction manuals.

We prefer to do a rush job even if there are some washers or nuts leftover. A man who wants to do the job right makes sure all nuts are used/exhausted. It took me a while to understand the different levels and peaks of intercourse. It took me just as long to become a less selfish lover. Studies say 1 in 3 women have difficulties reaching an orgasm. Why is that? I think it is a combination of women not understanding and being familiar with their bodies and men being inexperienced or lazy in their attempt to please their mate. Of course, there may be other medical variables or anxiety that is preventing climax. Whatever the case, most young adults do not discuss this, and there are some old adults with stinking thinking. I think it's pretty universal that during a person's early sex years—ages 17-21—the name of the game is the guy reaching maximum pleasure. However, that is all minor league thinking and behaviors.

After living in San Diego for a couple of years, I became the keyboardist for a local singing group, and that is how I met Destiny Jones. Destiny was desired by a few of my musician friends. She was the girl who everyone wanted a shot at but they were either too young or too scared to do anything about it. Destiny was 24-years-old when I met her, and I was 22. The advantage that I had is that I had only been in San Diego for a little bit, so she knew nothing about me, which prevented me from being lumped into the category of men that she considered boys. There is a term called "demonstrative communication," and that is when a person sends and receives signals without verbally speaking. Facial expressions, gestures, and body language can tell a person hello without actually talking. Destiny and I noticed each other, and I decided to be forward with her after three rehearsal sessions spent checking each other out from afar. After rehearsal one night, I approached her and said, "Hey, where are we going to eat after this?"

She gave a little smirk. "I don't know; it's late, nothing good is open."

I thought to myself, oh that's a nice way of turning me down, but then she said, "I live across the street. You can come over and chill if you want."

"Oh, I'm down for that."

Deep down I had butterflies. My first impression of Destiny was that she was probably used to guys who act "hard," and are slightly controlling. However, there was something about her that drew my interest. Destiny's flavor was chocolate cocoa. She was not petite; she was probably 5"7 with well-developed hips that would require two hands and a license to handle. Her butt was a distinct asset, accentuated in everything she wore, and this was before apple-bottom jeans and spandex leggings. Let's be honest, everybody wanted her face down, ass up in the air, doggy style. Bodies like this can be intimidating because you need to pack a lunch if sex is on the table.

I went to Destiny's house after the rehearsal and we got a chance to get to know each other. That is when most of my stereotypical thoughts were dispelled. Destiny was kind of a stylish geek with a lovely body. We made a strong connection that first night. We laughed and flirted; basically, we were setting the stage for a first real date. I had to read the situation correctly; she was not DTF (down to F**K) the first night, which was preferred because I do not get down like that on the first meeting either. I discovered that Destiny was a foodie and there was a restaurant in Coronado that she wanted to try.

At that point, I was half gentleman and half dog. I love to wine and dine, which I did, but I do not exclude women from treating the man. Our first restaurant experience was excellent. We laughed, we complimented each other, and we drank wine. I went back to her house, and the chemistry was high. Her place smelled fresh like a warm sweet bakery. Destiny and I drank more wine at her house, and flirted on the couch. We were feeling good and frisky. Her adorable geeky side was present as she was bashful to touch me. She had glasses on with her hair pulled back and she decided to slip into some little pajama shorts and a low-cut tee-shirt. As she walked back to the couch, I couldn't resist. Standing up and taking her by the waist, I pulled her in for our first kiss. My hands slipped from her waistline to her butt, and immediately I felt my penis bulging out of my pants because my excitement was peaking. I kissed her on the neck. Her breathing patterns changed, and then she said, "Follow me," leading me to her room.

I knew what time it was, but I still had doubts. She told me to get comfortable under her sheets, and I quickly noticed that she was able to set the mood. She lit some candles, and slipped off her pajama shorts, revealing a thong—the cakes on her were incredible. Her sheets and comforter felt different than my cheap ones at home. She jumped on the bed, and the kissing and touching resumed. Eventually, she pulled out a condom, but it was not a brand that I preferred. I wanted ultra-thin. I felt the pressure to perform, and everything was looking, smelling, and feeling right. She told me that she was ready—no need for foreplay—she wanted penetration. All of a sudden, I froze and started thinking about what type of connection we had. As I stalled, she started to get frustrated then asked, "Are you ready for this?" I said, "I don't know." Then all of a sudden something happened that I had never experienced or expected. Destiny went to her nightstand drawer and pulled out a dildo, turned on the vibrator, and started to pleasure herself right in front of me. My mouth dropped, as I was not sure if she was doing it for arousal or as a replacement.

Well, a couple of minutes later she made herself orgasm and I was on the outside looking in. The night passes, there's no shame in her game, and I'm thinking about how I'm going to recover from this collapse. What I did know, in spite of the unfinished ending, was that Destiny and I had a great night. The next week we went out again to another high-priced restaurant, but this time she paid. When Destiny paid it showed mutual investment and interest. It was evident we were enjoying each other's company, and we had chemistry. By that time, I was getting used to her, and all of my senses were kicking in, but most important, we were making an intellectual connection. We ended up at her house again and things got heated once again.

This time I had my overnight bag with my preferred condoms. One thing I admired about Destiny was that she was clean and cautious about safe sex. We ended up back on her bed, but this time I had a score to settle. I laid her down and kissed her all over. I had her completely naked, and kissed her stomach, making my way down, then abruptly she said, "I want you in me now." I swiftly strapped up and guided my penis inside of her. I could feel the walls of her pussy securing my dick, and both of us held our breath as we anticipated the moment. I'm on top of her but all I can think about is that ass and flipping it around, slapping it, squeezing it, and pounding into her chocolate fondue. I turned her around and, on the inside, I'm grinning, thinking about how I bet them other guys wish they were me.

As I am manhandling her waist, I'm throwing all of me into her, kissing her back and appreciating the art of her body. The sweat is breaking, and I'm noticing that both of us are ready for our heart rates to be racing until we reach our peak. I'm spending maximum time from behind because the view itself is enough for an 80-year-old man to get hard without the help of a pill. Finally, she asked to get on top and lays me back. As she rode my pole up and down, my fingers dug into her back as the moment intensified, then I started to go with her movement as my hands rested on her butt. Next thing I know, she's pushing herself lower onto me, and I can sense that something is about to happen. Suddenly, her moaning turns into OH's, followed by louder OH's! Her body is pulsating, and Destiny explodes. She starts ejaculating and lifts off my dick. A waterfall gushes out of her vagina, and she's rubbing her clitoris, shouting with pleasure. As her sprinkler system is going off I am thinking to myself, Welcome to The Big Leagues.

She was relieved and depleted. I expressed to her that I had never experienced that type of orgasm. "Have you?" I asked.

"That was the second time in my life," she replied.

Instantly, I patted myself on the proverbial back and

knew that hanging around with her meant I was headed for more good experiences.

I've always thought the best sex partners are the ones who masturbate and know exactly what pushes them to the edge. Of course, it's more exciting when your partner does what you want with a remix of their own style. Destiny and I continued to date, but we never said we were exclusive or operated under the umbrella of boyfriend and girlfriend. I felt we had an immense amount of freedom, yet we both had each other's undivided attention. She was quirky but daring, and I was attracted to her and those things.

Eventually, she moved in with her grandparents to help them out financially. Her grandparents were old fashioned, and she did not want to give the wrong impression about her dating life. I had dinner at their house a few times, but we were not comfortable about drifting off to her room. Destiny was a blue-collar type of girl—not very complicated, and a hard worker. She also wasn't the type who wanted to get frisky in the next bedroom over from her grandparents. Nor was she into hand jobs and oral sex; she was strict on just dick. There was a time late one night when we were both too lazy to drive to my house, so we went around the corner from her grandparents' house where there was a new housing development in the neighborhood. We parked in a cul-de-sac down a street with undeveloped homes.

I jumped out of my truck and went to the passenger side where I pulled her out and turned her around like a police officer about to frisk and arrest her. Well, I did frisk her from behind, then kissed her assertively. I reached around and unzipped her pants and pulled them down to her high heels.

It was cold and there wasn't much street light. She stood with the passenger door swung wide open and her body facing the seat covers. I would not let her turn around to face me; it slightly transformed into a controlling, role-playing scene led by me. I had her arms spread in a search and arrest position, but I didn't desire to take her to jail. I just wanted to take her for a ride.

Destiny was a bit nervous, and said that security patrolled this area to ensure there was no vandalism to the new homes. I immediately stuck one finger in her mouth to shut her up, and my other hand went to rub her clitoris. I kissed the back of her neck and applied more pressure to the right spots. Destiny could feel me pressing up against her ass from the back and she reached behind her back and unfastened my pants. She told me to get protection, then grabbed my hard stick and thrust it inside her. I instantly freed my hands up and elevated one of her legs onto the step of my truck, so one foot was on the pavement and the other in the truck. She arched her back for me just the right away, and slightly turned back, giving me *that* look. Her eyes and body language were saying, "Yes, you've got my ass in the air bouncing off of your pelvis, do what you want with it."

The setting was not ideal, but my adrenaline was racing through my body. I smacked her juicy chocolate ass just to hear the sound get lost in the night. She knew I wanted to dominate her, and she totally submitted. The feeling was so good I wanted to get as deep as possible inside of her. I had one hand on her pelvic bone, and the other on her shoulder, rooting myself deeper into her chocolate sea. I couldn't hold back anymore. I told her I was about to explode, and I pulled my dick out, ripped the condom off, and released all over the top of her ass. Destiny and I enjoyed that night, and many more. Our relationship was stable and peaceful. Our conversations were meaningful, but we never addressed long-term plans.

There was a level of depth that was missing, and we were too passive about the relationship, which ultimately became our demise. We slowly drifted apart; the flirtatious and dorky habits that I had adored were not enough to sustain us, and we failed to grow as a couple. I'm still confounded why neither of us ever said, "Hey, I want you to be mine." Though every experience has a purpose, and I suspect this one was to help in the development of my sexual stamina and appetite. Even though the relationship was drama free, it may have just been a lustful connection. Whatever the case, I will always respect her and appreciate the time we shared. I have seen her a few times over the years, and easiness and peace remains. Destiny made me take sex seriously, and elevated my level of knowledge and effort. However, being a marksman in the bedroom is not sufficient. The goal since then has been to be the maintenance man.

-III-

Consummating the Friendship

In seventh grade, I went to a new middle school, and out of 25 students in the class, I had the exact schedule for all seven classes with a girl named Marie Lopez. Marie and I both had braces on our teeth, and both looked trapped in that awkward adolescent phase. We did not speak that much. I was a young, black, preppy boy, and a competitive kid. She was a cute, young, Latino girl, but she was more interested in attracting the attention of white American boys. I had the best of all worlds. Growing up in San Bernardino County, I lived in East Highland—a predominantly Caucasian area. I had many white and Asian friends. Yes, I experienced prejudice, and have been called the "N-word," but it did not bother me because I figured if we lived in the same neighborhood, we had the same opportunities. (I realize now that's not accurate, but as a kid I was not going to feel inferior to anyone.)

While around my white friends, it was all love and fun. We'd play truth or dare, like I would with any group of friends. During one of those games in sixth grade, I kissed a white girl for the first time on the lips; her name was Audrey. The middle school I attended was predominantly Hispanics, and I adjusted well to that environment, building some of my best relationships with that group, but never learned Spanish. Well, only the bad words. The next city over was Rialto, which is where I had moved from, and my best friend Christopher still resided. When I wanted to be around the black culture, Rialto is where I went. In seventh grade, I was not trying to get involved with anyone, and friendship building was all that I cared about, nothing more. When I returned to the same school for my eighth-grade year, Marie and I again had the same schedule. By chance, we even selected the same electives, and one of them was yearbook.

It was in the eighth grade that Marie took a huge step forward into her young womanhood. Her braces were removed and she was out of the training bra. Marie was beautiful. That year, my relationship with Marie developed more, and we found each other quite comical. Even though she was attractive, I felt at the time that she needed a friend more than another guy sweating her. Other girls started getting jealous of her because it was obvious she was one of the prettiest girls at the school and probably had a stud for a boyfriend. I was popular and had a fan club as well, but a beautiful girl always supersedes the jock or captain of a team. A critical moment early in Marie and my friendship was when our peers booed her at the eighth-grade dance after being named queen. She ran out of the gym crying, and I followed to console her. I even caught flak from some of the black girls for doing so.

Yes, unfortunately, there's always racial tension, especially when it appears that the cream-of-the-crop is venturing into biracial dating. However, love is colorblind, and we often fall for those who reciprocate our affections. Marie was my friend, and I cared about supporting her when our classmates were unfair and cruel. Another friend and I walked her home that afternoon. Home for me was three and a half miles away from school, and from that day forward we walked home together more often than not for the rest of the school year.

Our friendship grew to the point where we were calling each other best friends all the way up to high school. In high school, Marie was officially FINE. I remember senior classman salivating over her when she was only a freshman. In high school I had my share of attention from the female sex. It was perceived as weird and unbelievable by our peers how close Marie and I had become without crossing the line. I was not the gay male friend who she went shopping with, nor was I the guy who was secretly hoping that she would see the potential in us. However, there were many times when Marie had bad break-ups in her relationships, and she would come over to my house and sneak into my room so I could hold her until she fell asleep in my arms. I admit this behavior was weird because my philosophy was, and still is, that a heterosexual man and woman cannot be true best friends because someone always ends up with the desire for more. Even then I suspected that if I kept emotionally supporting Marie she would eventually yield and compromise our friendship. Or if Marie kept jumping into my bed for me to console her, I might slip in a sympathy kiss while she was vulnerable. Surprisingly, that never came true.

We would ditch school and go swimming, or to the mountains, or movies. By our senior year, I was physically attracted to her, but programmed to just be her friend and not desire more. On one occasion, while I was at her house, her dad pulled me aside to thank me for being such a good friend to her throughout the years. Marie and I both won homecoming male and female awards, and had our share of love interests and heartache. Marie and I even ended up going to the senior prom together. Deciding to go to prom was a big deal because it is commonly an expectation that you will be romantically involved with your prom date. Guys were jealous and surprised that we decided to be each other's date. To be honest, I think it was her suggestion, but I knew the intention was just friendly, at least I thought.

At that point, the most Marie and I had ever done was peck on the lips and cuddle, but that was all under the umbrella of friendship. We both went all out for the prom event, and I was unsure about what to expect because I'd always known her as my friend, but I only knew prom night as a night of teenage sex. Marie was 18, and I was 17, and we decided to get a room at a resort in Palm Springs where the event was taking place. We never discussed expectation; we both just wanted to look good and have a superb time. At the prom, we danced with each other and danced with others, so there was still a friendship vibe hovering over our evening. She looked awesome in a red and black beaded, backless dress, hugging her hips. Her long dark hair was pinned up with curls falling around her smooth neckline leading down to flawless cleavage. We were looking good, feeling good, and riding in style in a black luxury SUV.

After prom, we all decided to head back to the resort to go night swimming. I did not drink in high school, so I didn't have any liquid courage, and knew that removing the friendship shield would put our friendship at risk. When we were in the hotel room changing, she got out of the shower with only a towel on and her hair dripping wet—the perfect setting. Naturally, my awkward teenage brain decided to say, "Hey, whatever you do, please don't let that towel drop or I may vomit." I was only joking, but it was the worst timing imaginatively possible. Marie laughed it off, but if she had been open to removing the friendship barrier that night, my comment had eliminated any hope of that happening. In my defense, I was young, sober, and did not know how to genuinely smooth-talk my best friend. We got into the pool with some friends, and one of our gay friends Rolando had issues that night and had not secured a room to stay over. Marie asked if he could stay with us, and I said, "Hell no!" We got into a little disagreement about it. Even though I knew there was not going to be any action between Marie and I that night, if I had agreed to Rolando sleeping in the room with us, the whole school would have known that I stayed in the "friend zone" all night. Rolando did find a room to crash in after all.

Marie and I slept together in the bed with our usual friendship cuddling on prom night. We did love each other as friends, and that was the most important part of our relationship. When I returned to school, everyone asked if I had gotten lucky with Marie. I told the truth that nothing had occurred, but they figured I was lying and just didn't want to share the details. They knew that Marie was attached to me at the hip, but it was our friendship that made it that way. After I graduated, I moved to San Diego to help and live with my sister who had a two-bedroom apartment. Marie moved with me to San Diego. For the first month, her parents could not believe it, but they trusted me to care for Marie. She moved back home after the summer ended.

During my first year in college, Marie and I remained close, but it was becoming a challenge to nurture our friendship parallel to our individual relationships with other people. One of the most difficult situations involved a girlfriend I had named Jasmine. We were working on maintaining a long-distance relationship. After an argument on the phone, Jasmine drove to my apartment and saw that Marie had an overnight bag in my room. (Marie was actually in town to go on a date with a guy she barely knew but needed to crash at my house as a contingency plan.) Jasmine became suspicious and upset and grabbed Marie's belongings then ran to the dumpster and emptied out Marie's things. I was enraged and worried about recovering Marie's things before she returned. Marie returned, and she could tell that something was wrong and said, "Hey I just need to get my stuff." Then Jasmine blurted out, "I threw your shit in the trash, bitch. It should *not* be in *my* man's room." Marie lunged to attack Jasmine. I had to separate them, and asked Marie to wait on the porch.

Just when I thought the situation was calming down, a brick came flying through the front room window. I ran outside in shock and yelled, "Marie, this is not just my house— my sister lives here too!" I could tell she was immediately remorseful. I just jumped in the dumpster, recovered the items to my best ability, and asked them both to leave. Marie's anger was justified, but not her actions. Our relationship eventually restored, and we continued to be friends through the years, but with less frequent visits. That incident helped me to realize how important it is for your spouse or significant other to like your friends, no matter their gender. Having to choose between a friend or a significant other is very emotionally difficult. At a minimum, they need to respect each other's role. If you want a dynamic, healthy relationship between your best friend and partner (that are the same sex), create opportunities for them to communicate without you being the middleman. (I know, easier said than done.)

Years ago, Southern California was on fire, and my neighborhood was evacuated. I drove to my parents, but then they got evacuated from their home. I decided to call Marie because I knew she had a place out of harm's way. She was happy to have me, and it had been a while since we had seen each other. The plan was to stay up a little bit, maybe have a glass of wine and watch a movie. We ended up watching Katt William's first standup comedy routine. I liked the fact that Marie was into black comedy because I'm diverse in my comedy selections, and I desired someone who was the same. Eventually, we headed to bed, but I was a little tentative because I was no longer that 17-year-old, sharing a bed with my girl buddy. Since the last time we had shared a bed I had some adult exchanges with some extraordinary women, particularly Destiny—the chocolate volcano. I did not trust myself to honor the friendship like I had in the past.

In addition to being more mature, Marie had made an alteration. She was in tip top shape with firm abs, a firm ass, and the bonus breast enhancements. I cannot say that breast enhancements are always an improvement, but self-confidence is attractive. If a person does something to raise their confidence level, then it is an overall improvement to that person. (And for the record, I would have taken Marie pre-breast enhancements.) We changed into our pajamas and dimmed the lights. As I was getting settled into my side of the bed, Marie leaned over to give me a goodnight kiss. The moment we touched lips, I could feel that it was different. Our lips were locked, but this time, our eyes were not open. Following the peck was a good mouth between lip kiss—the kind where her bottom lip rests between my lips, and I have the option to gently suck on her lip before slipping my tongue into her mouth.

Then came the moment where I couldn't help but think, are we doing this? My buddy, my friend. The pace started to pick up and she straddled me. I undid her pajama top to check out the goodie bags, then kissed her neck and breasts. When I flipped her around, our eyes met, and she said, "I don't know if we should." Being respectful of her and the friendship, I said, "We don't have to if the time isn't right." We held each other and went to sleep. The next day I headed out early. As I was driving back to San Diego, I started having regrets, and I sent her a text about how good everything had felt the night before and maybe we should entertain the idea of being more than just friends. Her response was she loved me back, but never addressed my plea. As time passed, I did not interpret her non-response as rejection. I figured we had made things confusing, and she felt retreating was the safest thing to do. In the meantime, we checked-in with each other from time to time but avoided talking about the proverbial elephant in the room.

Marie moved again. This time to a city 45-miles north of San Diego, and I happened to have an event to attend in her area. We made plans to have a night-cap at her house to catch up because I would not be able to make it to her house until 9 p.m. When I arrived, she already had a head start on the bottle of wine we planned to share. We were also just happy to see each other. The déjà vu thing is, we watched another comedy standup, but this visit she was more affectionate— lots of hugging early in the night, and there was a long period where she watched the show on my lap.

As we headed to her room at bedtime, I was thinking to myself, damn she looks good in her white satin undergarment. I was in the mood for the sweet mocha that she was serving, and I warned her, saying, "Hey, babe, you know our chemistry has picked up, and the way I'm feeling tonight may have you saying YES!" She decided to get in the shower, and in the interim, my mind was racing like Usain Bolt in a 200-meter competition. The crazy thing is we already loved each other and the familiarity with one another was off the charts. I know her scent, her touch, and her taste. Most importantly, I knew what she liked, and what she needed because I had been that constant friend in her life when things were right or wrong. I had unique insights on why things failed with her former relationships; I knew the things that they lacked. Yes, at times she is a princess, and she's accustomed to a man catering to her needs until their flexibility converts to a weakness. Marie did not need a guy that was going to smother her with attention. She needed someone who she could chase from time to time. The bottom-line, we loved each other, and the moment had finally presented itself where it was time to explore all feelings. After the shower, Marie approached my bedside.

"Why are you looking at me like you want me?" she said. "I thought you said if I drop this towel, you're going to vomit?

"Ha—Wow! You remember that!?"

"Oh, yes. You did kind of hurt my feelings."

"I'm sorry. I was young and did not know how to handle the moment."

"So, what is different now? So what, you have some chest hairs, and you're older."

"Well, now I know what I have in front of me. I misunderstood your delicacy and the unique possibility for what our friendship could grow into. Hey, but when I started feeling you, you did not have a response for me. Remember that?"

"This whole thing just makes me nervous, and I do not want to fuck up the purest friendship I have in this world."

"I feel the same. Let's just kiss and see if there are any sparks."

"No, Anthony, you don't have to play your little games with me. I love you, and tonight you can have anything you want."

Her words were music to my ears and heart, and gave me an instant erection. I could hear it in Marie's tone, and see it in her eyes that she wanted tonight to be different. The translation was, "Baby, I love you, and you may have me if this is what you want." I lowered her down to the bed where I was, and I gently kissed her on her lips. The passion level was high because we loved each other and our hearts agreed in that moment. I pulled my pants off. I wanted to show her how ready I was for this moment. She got even more excited as I laid her on her back then kissed and licked all over her body. I could feel that her pussy was moist and ready to receive me. I grabbed my penis, guiding it inside her.

Our eyes were locked on each other the entire time as I took my first couple of strokes inside of her. The experience was different on three levels. First, we were best friends crossing the line after so many years of being legit and withstanding. Second, her body was very fit—almost too perfect, and I found myself admiring it more than soaking in the anticipated moment. There was even a time I was pounding her from behind, and I caught myself smiling in the mirror. Lastly, I felt like Marie was more into satisfying me or just being connected than actually going sexually wild. I got on top of her again, and she caressed my back and chest. She said, "No condom; I want to feel your juices overflow inside of me." Everything was magnified. She rubbed my balls as I went deeper inside of her. She said all of the right things to get me to orgasm while digging deeper for the gold. It was so overwhelming that I lost my pace as I spilled into her Mexican flavored mocha canal. Her eyes filled with gratification and she said, "Honey, I didn't expect for you to be such a good lover." I kissed her and told her I loved her. She cleaned up, and we held each other as usual, falling asleep.

The next morning, I had to leave early, and even though we crossed the line of friendship, there was an unspoken mutual understanding that things would remain the same.

Neither of us were looking to pursue a life together. I think we both realized that we already had the best part of each other. We already had each other's heart, care, and respect. Surprisingly, the sex did not dilute our connection, it made it even more secure. Our experience demonstrated to me that we were friends who were willing and comfortable enough to open ourselves up to unknown possibilities because we loved and trusted each other that much.

I pose the question, is it best to marry your best friend? Not all people are looking for that, right? Christine Cook's famous quote says, "Marriage is getting to have a sleepover with your best friend, every single night of the week." I ask, how do we pick our friends? My guess would be a high percentage of us select friends due to proximity. We grew up in the same neighborhood, had the same school instructor, or shared the same family friends. Another percentage of friendships form due to being involved in the same activities or having similar interests, such as both people enjoy hanging out in a jazz lounge or at the theater. Friends are often selected by chance, and from there a bond begins to grow. Wedding your best friend does not always present as the best choice, though. I think the business side of a marriage is underrated and sometimes overlooked.

I have always had a set of rules concerning what would make a good marriage for me. Anthony's four P's for a successful relationship: peace, pleasure, prosperity, and partnership. The first 2 P's are easy to accomplish as close friends. If the person is your best friend, they know the things that irk you, down to what groceries not to bring home. Your best friend's temperament is likely to be compatible with yours, and that's why they have remained your best friend. Pleasure can be tricky, but still very obtainable between best friends. Pleasure can come in the form of sex or the shape of a love language, such as a gift. The business side of things addresses prosperity and partnership. It is harder to find a friend who shares the same ambition and work ethic as you. In many cases, we have best friends who give life and financial advice too. It's okay to respect their advice and love them because of what they mean to you. However, sharing secrets is incredibly different than sharing the same credit report.

The truth about this argument is that it all depends on what side of the spectrum you are operating from. For example, optimistic lovers, especially the people who plan on only marrying once, are often looking for a two-for-one deal. Having a best friend and a spouse rolled into one is viewed as ideal. For the pessimistic lovers—and individuals on their second marriage or who are iffy about marriage altogether—it may be perceived as being too dangerous to risk losing both their best friend and spouse in one breakup. After the divorce, whose couch are they supposed to crash on? There is no right or wrong answer. People form lifelong romantic relationships for many reasons. Whether it is your best friend or not, it takes a tremendous amount of work. Marie and I had a love connection, but the strong friendship we had developed over the years wouldn't allow even romance to detour what was meant to be; best friends.

-IV-

You're 33 and a Virgin? Oh Boy!

Years ago, I was asked to provide music for a weekly Friday night event for a friend. They needed me to be the lead keyboardist, and work with the lead vocalist. When I met the vocal leader Ashley Rose, I could tell she was used to being in control, and accustomed to others following her orders. Ashley was older than me by at least five years, and she had this astute, secretary-type look—the nerdy, sexy kind that wears designer reading glasses and a pin to keep her hair up. She was average looking at first glance, but almost seemed like she was in disguise, hiding another side to herself. Ashley was half white & half Mexican, with some urban culture texturing her personality. The more we worked together, the more I became fascinated by her, and that fascination drew me in even more because she was really into my craft. I even caught her mesmerized by my playing a few times. It is an awesome feeling when somebody digs the artistic side of you. An artist can be very vulnerable with their work and performance. Even seasoned professionals have moments of insecurity and need heartfelt appreciation from their audiences. I liked that she was methodic in her selections and shy about how good she was. The music was bringing us closer, and an undercurrent of attraction began to develop.

After one event, I commented about noticing that she didn't tend to hang out with anyone outside of our practice sessions and performances. "I'm interested in getting to know the other side of you," I said. She giggled, but it was almost more of a knowing laugh like, Mister, you do *not* know what you are getting yourself into. We all went out as a group, but Ashley and I ended up sitting next to each other and used a majority of the time for one-on-one conversation. At the end of the night, she sent me a text message asking if I could talk on the phone. It was a late evening, but I was a young bachelor and had no other plans for the night. I called, and as we talked our connection continued to grow, but the innocence of the conversation quickly shifted. Ashley had been sheltered in her youth and had never experienced a serious relationship, and she was almost 30 years old. Her parents raised her to be very conservative and to follow God. She put most of her attention on her work and family and had never nurtured a personal relationship. Ashley was introverted but was very curious about romance. Instead of laughing or running away, I thought this was very different; an older woman with no experience. On the phone that night she revealed that she was interested in me but had insecurities about showing me all aspects of her.

"What about you are you scared to share?" I asked.

"I have a very inquisitive mind, and I think about how intimate things, such as sex will feel - like a lot."

"Wow, I do not even know what to say. I can tell that you are a passionate person. What is it about sex that consumes your thought?"

"The idea of another person touching my body, kissing my body, and pulling sounds out of me that I did not even know I could make. These thoughts excite me a lot."

"Whoa, Ashley, it is getting late, and you just took my mind down a street that is dangerous; we should probably conclude this phone call."

"No, did I just excite you or something?"

"Yes."

"See, it excites me knowing that I excited you. What do you like to do when you get excited by yourself?"

"Damn girl, why are you taking us there?"

"Hey, I warned you that there was another side to me. So what is it about me that you like?"

"I do like that you are intelligent and appear to have multiple layers to your personality."

"No, Tony, cut the crap—what is it about my appearance that you like?"

"I think you have an attractive librarian type of look, like you're hiding a naughty girl."

"Oh, do you like naughty girls? Do you like girls who let you squeeze their nipples and rub your cock?"

"Hmm, yeah."

"I'm squeezing my nipples right now for you."

"Oh, are you? Are you doing anything else?"

"What else do you want me to do?"

"I want you to put your hand down your panties—"

"I'm not wearing any panties."

"Oh, my, I want you to touch down underneath your hood and check the oil. Is it wet for me?"

"Yes, it is. I want you to check your stick shift and get ready to change the gear for me…"

I couldn't believe our *first* phone conversation led to phone sex. Ashley had me thinking about her all weekend, thinking to myself *this nerdy little freak.* After a couple of late night conversations, we decided that I would come over and watch a DVD with her. She lived alone in a lovely two-bedroom condo. Because she was an interior designer, Ashley's house was coordinated very well. This is cool, I remember thinking—a grown woman, intelligent and independent, but with the sexual experience of a teenager. She only had one TV, though, which was in her bedroom. The other kicker was that she had rented the movie *White Chicks.* I thought that was funny because I was watching it with a white girl. As we laughed during the film, we shared popcorn and cozied up on her bed. She had pajama shorts on—very relaxed, and there was some light touching, but nothing too erotic.

As soon as the movie ended, we started making out. I kissed her, and my hands were caressing her back. She got on top and straddled me; she was very excited. I thought maybe even more excited than normal because this side of her was untapped. For the first time in maybe a long time, she had someone who was showing interest in getting through her barriers. I took off her bra while she was on top of me. While kissing me, she said, "Oh, I can feel your dick getting hard through your pants."

I replied, "My rule is not to take it out unless it's going to get wet." She's moaning like an eager, freckled-face teenager with braces experiencing something for the first time. Then suddenly, the movie credits stopped rolling, and the room fell silent. She stopped abruptly, stood up and said, "Sorry, you have to leave now." I was like, "What is the problem?" She said, "This is a mistake, you must go." As I gathered my shoes, she rushed me out of the house so quickly that I did not even get a chance to put my shoes on until I reached the porch. I thought to myself, oh, I see why she does not have a man, but I did not take that moment as rejection. I took that moment as her rejecting her inexperienced side. She was scared to explore the moment; she was not afraid of me.

For the next couple of weeks she shunned me until she completely withdrew from participating in the weekly events. I was not too bothered about our disconnection. I was, however, surprised to run into her years later while working on a community project together. We were both tasked to help with the branding of an organization as we both had marketing backgrounds. When Ashley and I reunited, there was not much awkwardness. I had moved on and flushed that strange memory down the toilet. What was evident was that she and I worked very well together, and after months of hard work we were able to come up with a finished product. During that process, our minds linked up so much that we started admiring each other in a new way. At one point, we were in the studio working on a commercial, and we were in the room alone for quite some time. I could tell that it was making her nervous. I think she got to the point where she didn't trust herself to be alone with me. We had both underestimated our intellectual chemistry, and I was very impressed by the deeper view of her creative imagination that working together again had given me. This experience may have been the first time that I was amazed by the emotional and intellectual layers of a woman.

When working side by side with someone, after a while, you can tell why they are single, happy, or unhappy. We all have had bosses who were just mean people. Mean female bosses get labeled as being a bossy bitch who just need some dick. Mean male bosses get their kicks on being in power and abusing their position of authority. We know what it feels like to have incompetent coworkers and have to repeat instructions of a task over and over again. After working with Ashley, what I gathered was that she was single and a virgin for so long because of three things. First, she had some self-confidence issues. I do not think she felt secure enough to share intimate secrets or talents with anyone of the opposite sex. She wore suits and skirts to play the professional part but deep down inside she did not shy away from blue collar work, such as working on a car with her dad. Ashley did not view herself as a sexual being, probably because of her conservative and religious upbringing. Ashley lacked public sexuality, but with me, she was interested in discovering it.

Second, she lived in her head too much. When you are constantly living in your head, you talk yourself out of opportunities and risks. Self-doubt loves to fester in the minds of people who have issues with self-confidence. I think it is everyone's goal to find someone who will accept the dorky, quirky, weird, and embarrassing side of themselves. Ashley was a very passionate person and needed someone who could nurture her passions. Lastly, Ashley required practice and experience with day-to-day interactions between herself and available men. Somehow, she had missed some crucial lessons that most people learn in their adolescent years. She had not even experienced heartbreak. Never having a broken heart is emotionally equivalent to not having chickenpox as a child and ending up with shingles as an adult.

In the studio that night, I told Ashley I had enjoyed working with her, and that it had been a very positive experience because we made a great team. I quickly learned that she appreciated positive reinforcement because she lit up with gratitude. We hugged, and while pulling away from the embrace, we kissed. The kiss was somewhat accidental and in the moment, but passionate. It meant a lot to us that we were able to complete a massive project together while maintaining professionalism and admiring each other's ability. Many couples cannot even bake cookies together without disagreeing about whether to use butter or margarine. Just as we finished kissing, the studio engineer walked in, and he could tell that something had happened between us. He just laughed to himself. Admittedly, it was written all over our faces, and the passion was still evaporating from the room. As we left the studio, Ashley called me, and she wanted to meet me in a convenience store parking lot. She confessed that her feelings for me had reignited and she was hoping that we could explore those feelings if it was mutual. I told her that I did like her, but I was hesitant because of how things had ended so abruptly before. However, on that night, I could feel her desire and an earnest plea to give it a shot. I could not deny that there were common feelings. She grabbed me while standing in the parking lot and kissed me - a reassurance that this is what she wanted.

Ashley and I started talking again; this time around it was more balanced. I learned about her passions, fears; and just the depth of her desires to be great at something. She trusted me and appreciated my responses and humor. Soon after, we established a routine of talking daily; her sexual curiosity appeared again. She told me she was 33 and still a virgin, but not just to sex—oral sex, nude body touching, and even to being in love. One thing that drew me to Ashley was that she would email me daily, poignant descriptive letters about how she was falling for me and how happy she was about us. Emotionally, we shared a lot in our exchanges. I think because she was scared of prior rejection, I kind of cherished her feelings a bit more and handled her with care. I started evaluating the magnitude our relationship and looking at it from every angle. If I was her first experience with all of these things and she liked it, she could get addicted to me, or at least addicted to the feelings that I gave her.

Ashley became very interested in entertaining the sex conversation again. I told her that I would take on the hat as the teacher and she loved the idea of submitting to me. Her sexual hunger was officially roaring and ready to be fed. I would warm her up over the phone and tell her what things to expect, but I wasn't as worried about her performance because I knew this was going to be a passionate experience for me. Sometimes passion can overtake performance. Ashley got a rush from being sexual in public places; she wanted to start her "student training" in unexpected places. I remember our first "lesson" was after a rehearsal I had. She surprisingly showed up to the venue and parked next to my truck. As I was walking to my vehicle, she demanded for me to follow her. We went to a public park; it was late at night, and I jumped into her SUV when we arrived. She had music playing, and was wearing lingerie under her long coat jacket.

As I got into the car, she was happy to surprise me, and she was feeling naughty. We started to kiss, and she unfastened my pants from the driver seat. She said, "I want to do a good job sucking your dick. I want to taste all of you." She asked me, "What makes a person good at sucking dick?" I took the question in fun, but she was serious and role playing as a student. I said, "What I'm going to teach you tonight are fundamentally sound principles that should work across the board." (No, I have never sucked a dick or even had a thought of doing that. However, I have had some good experiences in that area, and had discussions with many male friends about other females sucking skills.) I told Ashley it is not that complicated but even simple things can get screwed up. Open communication between the parties is the real key to success when it comes to oral sex or any sexual activity. Preference varies for different men, of course, and learning how to communicate and take cues from your partner will bring satisfaction.

The main three things are a balanced mix of technique, attitude, and swallowing. (Remember, I am not trying to turn her into a porn star.) When it comes to a balanced blend, for me, there needs to be a combination of jacking off the base of the penis and suction of the head of the penis. Mouth lubrication and friction are essential when handling a hard dick. Attitude is important for people who are sensitive to their partner's emotional responses, and are driven by sound, like myself. I need you to want to suck my dick and tell me how bad you want to, and how bad I need it to be done by you. If it seems like a chore, the vibe will be that you're not trying to please me; instead, you're just trying not to lose me or hear me complain. Sucking dick may seem demeaning to some, but it is a very intimate exchange that can bring a couple closer together in more ways than physical. It is also especially arousing when your sex partner submits to being your sex slave. However, the domination and feeling of being in control should be reciprocated when the guy is performing oral sex on a female. If the girl wants to shove my face in her pussy and not let me up for air, I'll take the abuse in return.

Finally, all guys love it when they have the option to ejaculate wherever they may please. I love when a girl says, "Where do you want to cum?" The mental picture of ejaculating in your mouth, on your face, or your breasts makes the oral experience more fulfilling. Like a good student, Ashley was taking mental notes. She pulled my penis out in her car, and the first thing she did was squeeze my penis firmly like she'd been dreaming about being face-to-face with it. I was excited, and didn't want to talk throughout the process. The selfish side of me was coming out, and I just wanted to plant my seeds in her mouth, knowing I would be the first one ever. (I felt like Johnny apple seed.) She told me she wanted to do a good job. I said, "Just express the way you feel about me through this action." Right away, she started sucking my dick, making sounds like I had just delivered a Vince Lombardi pregame speech. I'm feeling good as she marinates my cock in her mouth, gently stroking me at the same time. I unclasped her bra and started to rub her breast with one hand while caressing her hair with the other. Ashley suddenly stopped, and in a sexy tone she said, "I want you to bite my nipples, and she started rubbing her vagina as I nibbled on her breasts. She was a B-cup, which can be a firm, fun size, as hers were. She started getting more aggressive and said, "I want to fit all of you in my mouth, and I want you to pull my hair down into your lap and make me do a good job." She was starting to become the teacher's pet already.

Ashley started sucking on me again and she found the right combination. She was sucking and massaging my penis, and she would say in between breaths, "Please let me taste your cum, I want it now." It did not take long for me to warn her that I was about to cum. She started moaning for it, and as I began to release in her mouth my toes flared, and my body tensed up like she was taking *my* virginity, and she swallowed it all. Without a flinch. The funny thing is that usually I wouldn't kiss a girl after oral on me, but I knew I had to set the correct tone, and she didn't know the formalities, so I kissed her on the lips and said, "Good, baby." Her skills were actually legit right out of the door. She made me feel like we were acting out one of her fantasies. She received a B+ from me. An A+ performance requires the girl to suck on my balls while jacking me off from underneath.

It is challenging in a relationship when one partner has had more erotic experiences than the other. I think it is good to know what your partner is used to because, no matter what, their mind will go back to the good ol' days. Most people started their sexual journey on a fairly average, common scale. Like your first dining experience was at Denny's or Sizzler.

However, we all advance, hopefully, then we start to eat at fancy restaurants on the pier or in the city—restaurants with menu items we cannot pronounce or places where the menu does not have an actual dollar price. Instead it reads "Market Price." Yes, our taste buds *and* our sexual appetite evolves. Just like it would be difficult for your partner to drag you back to Denny's after eating lobster on the pier, it's hard to go from a girl who lets you orgasm wherever you want to a person who is grossed out by sperm. I am not saying it's impossible to be in a happy relationship with someone who has more sexual restrictions (because you can't always say yes to everything); however, being equally yoked in the bedroom can help to keep your partner's mind from wandering.

I was looking forward to more experiences with Ashley, but honestly, I was catching strong feelings for her. Ashley was smart and cute, and made me feel special as the man who understood her. It did not take much time for Ashley to get addicted to my reactions. When a woman gets a man to climax, the guy has a big reaction (well, at least I do). She had never made a man feel sexually pleased, giggly, exhausted, or horny. My responses to her sex acts gave her a sense of empowerment, achievement, and control. My positive reaction boosted her self-esteem. Ashley was aiming to be my best experience, and she wanted to give me oral sex *all* of the time. I never got tired of meeting up with her so she could perfect her performance.

During our oral sex splurge, Ashley moved in with her parents because her dad was sick and she was changing careers. One time, she asked me to meet her halfway at a hotel, and we booked a suite. This was the night she wanted me to take her virginity and we wanted it to be memorable. This was the first time I felt like a female wanted me to take her virginity. In the sense that she wanted me to control and rule over her body. Even though she was freely giving her body to me, her fantasy was to be dominated and desired. As we got settled into the room, we acknowledged that we cared about each other deeply and belonged to one another, although the title boyfriend and girlfriend was never said.

There was a hot tub in the front room and this was the first time I got a look at her completely naked body. I got in the tub first while she was in the bathroom changing. She was always seeking my approval, and as she exited the bathroom, completely naked, she said, "I hope you like the way I groomed." She had a Brazilian bikini wax (with the landing strip), and as she stepped into the tub, she looked like a mature, sexy woman. She let her hair down. She had nice breasts and childbearing curves—she was half Latino and she had some shape to her butt. Ashley got into the tub, and I took her glasses off, pulling her down to me as we started kissing.

She started rubbing my dick under water, and I was just too anxious to be inside of her. She said to me, "I'm ready to take my final today, Professor." I pulled her out of the tub and laid her on the bed. Spreading her legs open, I said, "It's time for me to do some more teaching." With the tip of my tongue, I licked and kissed her clitoris. I took my fingers and spread the lips between her hips as I pushed my tongue deeper into her. She started to breathe heavier, and I cuffed her butt cheeks in each hand as I began to partake in all of her virgin margarita. The more she moaned the deeper I drank from her fountain. After 33 years, she was finally ready. We had connected socially, emotionally, and intellectually. Ashley found a friend in me, and a person who was going to be patient, understanding, and okay with her hidden emotions and outlook on life. I was ready for the moment. I slid up to her face, and she asked me, "Do you love me?" I said yes because I did. Though she did not need to hear it because she could feel it through my patience and unwavering effort to try to understand her. I grabbed my hard penis and I squeezed it inside of her. She was a little uncomfortable, but she was ready to press through the pain. I was gentle in the beginning, but as the session progressed I gave her what she wanted. She wanted to be pounded on top and from behind.

I controlled her from behind, smacking her ass. She wanted me to slap it hard to the point where she could see my hand imprinted on her butt cheeks. I stroked her from the back and reached my hand around to rub her clitoris while my dick slid in and out. I was biting her back and I could feel her Horchata juice running down to my testicles. As the arousal grew, I asked her if she wanted to get on top, but she was timid, and I didn't take offense when she declined. She enjoyed my lead and wanted me to keep giving it to her from the back. Ashley then asked me to cum on her face. I pulled my dick out and released my sperm on her face, like she wanted—to feel degraded. We both got what we wanted: I got a passionate, submissive virgin, and she got nailed like a slut. Her fantasy was to be loved and desired, but her hidden side wanted me to exhibit sexual domination over her. From that point forward, the sex took on a personality of its own. She became obsessed—not just with sex, but with being sexually subservient to me.

Ashley and I continued to hang out and talk, but sex was always expected. I did not have any complaints, but at one point I was worried that she may want a baby or something more that I was not willing to commit to at that time. We needed to slow down. She wanted sex all the time, and location was never an obstacle. She'd have me pull over in random neighborhoods—day or night—wanting to have sex in the backseat in front of strangers' houses. Eventually, she got comfortable straddling me in the car, smothering my penis until I came inside of her. We started using protection because I was not ready for a life-long commitment. Then the day came when I had to tell her no. Ashley wanted me to commit more to the relationship, but there was an age gap, and we were in two different places in our lives.

Less than a week later, it caught me by surprise when one day she just changed her phone number, cutting me off abruptly, like the initial time when she had kicked me out of her condo. There was a side to Ashley that would quickly retreat and withdraw feelings. It was a problem for Ashley that she had given me so much of her, but we were not on the same page regarding the future and timelines concerning our relationship. Ashley started to come emotionally undone. She would call me at sporadic hours of the night from unknown numbers. If I happened to answer, she would demand that we meet, and I would because I was concerned about her. We would get together and she would be dejected until we completed a sexual deed. Then she would disappear again. I realized she wanted to regain control over her life and our relationship. Ashley wanted things to be on her terms and me being a sexually weak man, she knew I would make myself available when she wanted a sexual fix. I wasn't entirely mature enough or focused enough to handle the roller coaster of Ashley that I had helped to create.

Unfortunately, Ashley's father passed in the process. I was sad and regretted that I was not in her support corner to aid her in that difficult time. More than a year passed after that before she reached out to me again. When she did, we met up in a public setting, and by then she had transformed a bit. She had picked up some weight, became more extroverted, and seemed nonchalant about life. I could tell she was still dealing with a lot of pain from the passing of her father, and the fact that we had not had any closure between us. The person who she loved and had given her treasured jewel to had disappointed her. We were able to laugh and flirt, but I was not going to allow her to suck me back into her web of confusion. Ashley was in a new place, and I could see how I had contributed to the new her. I won't go so far as to say that the new her is not the best her, because maybe she is content with her life. I do not know how long it is going to take for someone else to penetrate her heart again. I think I was the type of love that she was waiting for, but it did not come on her terms or timing. When I did a follow-up with Ashley she was still seeing a shrink and unpacking our issues on the therapist's couch. At that point in my romance journey, Ashley was definitely my strongest intellectual connection. I often wonder if she wishes she had never met me at all (because of the conditions I left things in).

It was not until much later, after deep reflection, that I began to understand the true issues that lived within the depths of Ashley. Ashley presented herself as an introvert who was inexperienced to dating or anything sexual with the opposite sex. I treated her accordingly, while not knowing that I was entertaining maybe something more hidden. Ashley said she was a virgin, but after calculating everything that happened, the math did not add up. Ashley was likely hiding another side of herself. This side wanted to be sexually dominated, and when her wishes were granted there was never a sign of unbearable pain. Once again, Ashley never flinched at an idea presented or an action made towards her. Ashley did not mind being degraded or treated like a sexual object. She was fixated on rough and punishing sex. The worst thing I could have done was feed into her condition through role play as the instructor and Ashley as the student. Ashley probably faced sexual abuse somewhere in her life and as a result identified with a particular type of sexual interaction.

Was Ashley a Virgin to sex? I do not know for sure, but I do know she was a virgin to healthy love and pure-hearted sexual encounters. Our relationship not working did not cause her to see a therapist, someone had already tampered with Ashley's emotional responses to relationships. Meanwhile, I thought I was the savior, the guy who was giving this inexperienced girl some attention—how kind of me to break down her barriers and get her to open up. The breaking down of her walls falls somewhere between detrimental and useless if I cannot identify with the root of her issues and apply the right tools. There are many women with Ashley's story, and it is important to be able to determine if a person is a healthy sexual freak or hurt sexual freak. Looking back, I think I encountered the latter, and if I had known I would have loved her differently.

-V-

The Deal I Couldn't Close

There should be growth from relationship to relationship; growth in the thought process, decision-making, and self-awareness. It is normal for guys or girls to freeze up when they see a highly attractive person or someone they perceive as being "out of their league." In my younger years, I let my lack of confidence, and resulting lack of assertiveness, allow beautiful women to slip through my fingers. To achieve self-growth, it is important to approach situations carefully until the individual conquers the fear and attains self-satisfaction. When a man wants something, he should overcome his fears and go after what he wants. Men are hunters, and we will try every clever trick in the book to capture our game. In my opinion, there is a great percentage of women who are single because men do not step up to the plate to even attempt a hit for fear of a strike out. I am all for the man who at least takes a swing because he showed courage and understands that rejection is part of the nuances of dating and finding the right person.

Unfortunately, some people get rejected by the opposite sex, and the rejected person starts to dish out insults because their feelings are hurt, or they feel embarrassed. Growing up, my best friend Christopher refused to approach girls unless the girl put it in writing that they would agree not to reject his advances. In social settings, while trying to find a new friend or potential dating partner, vulnerability and courage are essential traits to possess. On one particular occasion, I pushed my courage to the limit.

When I was around 26-years-old, two co-workers and I decided to go to a popular lounge in North Park, California. My friend Franklin had just received a huge promotion, and we were going out to celebrate. Both Franklin and my friend Mike were half Asian and White. Mike was an introvert and Franklin was an extrovert, and neither of them were my ideal wingman. It was a Thursday night, and we all had to be up by 5:30 a.m. for work the next day. The plan was to meet at the lounge around 10 p.m. and call it a night by 12. We celebrated at a shared table with some girls. The place was very crowded, and I was engaged in small-talk with an attractive girl who was married but enjoying her ladies' night out. I am easy going in a conversation—remember my friend Lawrence who always accused me of taking up too much time in conversations with one girl, rather than getting multiple numbers? Anyway, as the night was slipping away, two girls walked in, and the entire club paused.

Both girls had a presence, style, and beauty that could

stop traffic. Guys who were in a conversation immediately fell silent. This lounge had a cover charge after 9 p.m., and I'm 100% sure these women walked in for free. They were so attractive that if the lounge had been at maximum capacity, the security team would have thrown out four paying customers to make sure these non-paying ladies got into the building. I smirked, watching men who had been flirting all evening with different girls try to free themselves up so they could take a shot at the new stand-outs. Many men have a pure predator instinct, and when they see something better they want to make sure they are not caught giving another women attention which could potentially hinder their chances with the better choice.

Women, however, are often much smoother. If they are in conversation and someone more appealing enters the room they just dismiss themselves and go to the restroom, not returning to that spot in the club. Luckily, I was in a friendly conversation all night and was free to roam without commitment or guilt. And I wanted a shot at this particular girl who I'd been drawn to since the moment she walked in. She was stunning, and for the first time, my competitive nature and desire overrode my fear. The room became so competitive, though, it was a peculiar predicament. First, I could not tell what nationality this girl was. I also understand that not all people are into African American men, which is fine. Preference is okay, but stereotyping with a racial prejudice is not. However, I am confident in my personality and in navigating my way through a mature conversation with any woman. But if a person does not entertain a particular race, it's not worth the time to pursue.

For example, if a Latin or European woman said to me, "Sorry, I am not attracted to African American men in a romantic way," that is fine. I will not spend my evening arguing or trying to convince the person or group that they are wrong. Saying that I do not date white girls is different from saying that I do not date smokers. I would be excluding/discriminating against someone because of their skin color, which is dramatically different than an unattractive social habit. People are superficial, and this goes for all races. Everyone is not open to trying something new, and some people do not understand that beauty goes deeper than skin complexion. So entering into a conversation with the goal to advance can be difficult sometimes when the person is not the same race as yourself. There are places I can go and know that the individuals in the room are attracted to all races, but the place where we were was diverse, and it was not so obvious if a black man was on an equal playing field. However, the one thing that is universal, and can overcome all biases, is confidence and positive energy. If a person possesses these two things, they have a shot with any single person in the room. The second issue for me was that these girls, particularly the one I liked, were getting flooded with attention from all types of men and staff members in the lounge.

I watched guys bring the ladies drinks unsolicited just to engage in conversation with them. Some of the men looked like high rollers, and some looked suspect. I decided to be "me" and get creative so I could be in the mix. I saw the girls walking through the crowd of people dancing, and I positioned myself in front of the woman I liked. We were all doing the shuffle while trying to get through the crowd, and as soon as I felt that she was directly behind me I abruptly turned around and said to her face with disdain, "Did you just grab my butt?" She started laughing in disbelief and said no. I said, "Come on, you just got a handful of my butt cheek, and that's not okay. You can't just go around touching anyone's ass without asking for permission just because you are nice-looking." I walked away and gave her a not-so-happy look before she could reply.

Yes, this was all strategic on my part; I needed an encounter with her, but I also wanted to create a scenario where there was one person in the lounge who was not giving her "princess" treatment. As silly as it sounds, I made myself into the victim and her into the villain. The bonus surprise to our encounter was she had a thick Australian or British accent. I let 10 minutes go by, then I purposely made our paths cross again in the lounge. As soon as we made eye contact, I made an X with both index fingers, as in *stay away from me*. She immediately approached me, trying to plead her innocence.

The plan was going better than expected because it bothered her that I saw her in an unpleasant light. I waited another 20 minutes before taking a vacant seat next to her at the bar. It was a perfect opportunity to engage before another guy pounced on her. I approached her and said, "Even though you violated my personal space I am willing to make amends." I also said, "Hi, my name is Anthony, and you are?" She replied, "Hanna," but with her accent it was way cooler and pronounced like "Haw-na."

I said, "You have an enticing accent, and the way you commanded every man's (and some women's) attention when you entered the room was quite remarkable. I wonder, why do women like you even walk into a club or bar with a wallet? You never get a chance to use your money because all these men are desperate to buy you a drink."

Hanna replied in a sarcastic and snub kind of way, "Well then, where is my drink?"

"I'm sure you could get a bunch of these chumps to buy drinks for all three of us," I replied. "Yes, that's how good you both look."

Hanna cracked a smile and laughed.

"So what is your friend's name?" I asked. "She has a very exotic look, and you have a classy, adult, and sexy attraction."

"Thanks, her name is Tonya."

"Okay, I understand by me continuing to talk to you that I'm holding up the line for other guys to buy you and Tonya free drinks, so why don't we skip the shenanigans and let me have your number so I can get to know you and we can discuss how you can make it up to me for grabbing my butt earlier."

Hanna giggled. "I like your boldness. How about you guess our nationality and maybe I'll give you my number."

"I am terrible at this kind of stuff, but I'll try. You have this urban flavor to you, but your hair and complexion are too light for you to have any black in you. Do you have some Puerto Rican in you? Maybe Tonya is black and something or Persian heritage?"

"Sorry. Wrong, wrong, wrong. Nice playing with you, goodbye."

"No, please just tell me."

"Tonya is half African American and Filipino. I have

Dutch, French, and Australian. Yes, I have a blend of good, wonderful, and marvelous. Now, quit being cheap and buy us a drink."

"Why? You have untouched glasses of alcohol right in front of you. Paid for, courtesy of some hardworking chump."

"So what? I appreciate the gesture and enjoy watching these desperate men spend. Oh bloody, just kidding."

"Ha! You said bloody. That accent and dialect increases your score in my book."

"Oh, and what score do I have out of 10?"

"Hmmmm…like a 9.25."

"Oh, BULL SHIT! The way your eyes are popping out of your head is telling me otherwise. And your damn stuttering makes me feel like an 11."

"Ha ha. Hey, you can get that ten if you just give me your number because cooperation goes towards the overall score as well. Plus, I have to leave and be responsible so that I can wake up early for work tomorrow."

"Damn, you're persistent."

"I'm just trying to make a new friend."

"Okay, then why don't you just give me your number?"

I felt a slight kick to the gut as soon as she said that dreadful phrase. When a woman opts to take the guy's number instead of offering up their own that generally means they are not that into you. Yeah, I may have been slightly out of my league, but Hanna and I were connecting. I was able to hold her attention for at least seven minutes. And I did not want to come off too anxious and push the issue for her number because that is a turnoff. Sadly, there are hopeless and sneaky guys who will take a girl's phone and act like they are going to input their number, but instead call themselves from her phone so they can deceitfully acquire her number. Now, to me, a move like that is for the low-life, and I will never do anything like that, unless it is Beyoncé Aniston or Halle Johansson. I ended up giving Hanna my number, but my confidence had diminished significantly; I felt like I had lost a game of tug-of-war. Hanna and I went back and forth for a few more moments, but I walked away with rope-burned hands after falling on my ass. I said bye to Hanna and Tonya and proceeded to exit the lounge with my friends. It's funny because another way to tell that a girl is not going to engage anymore with you is by watching how the friend(s) respond or react. And Tonya had looked at me like I was not a contender.

Just as we made it to the door, I told Franklin and Mike that I'd meet them outside; I had unfinished business. I marched back to Hanna, and they could see me coming. They paused their conversation as I approached, and gave me that "Now what" look.

"Excuse me, I hate to bother you two again, but something is not sitting well with me, and I just cannot leave on this note."

"Oh bloody, what is it?"

"See, I want to get to know you, but I feel like your night is just going to progress as per your usual and we are never going to talk again after I leave."

"Sorry, honey, you're losing me; I do not know what you mean."

"After I leave you're going to have a few more drinks, which may result in you forgetting my name."

"No, I won't, Anthony."

"Well, my name is common. Look on your phone. I did. How many Anthony's do you know? How are you going to be able to tell which Anthony I am after I leave, and after a few more drinks?"

Hanna pauses, contemplating.

"How are you going to know this Anthony from the other Anthony's? Huh? Oh, I know how."

"How? "

"I'm the Anthony who kissed you." As soon I uttered those words I leaned in and kissed her on the cheek. That was risky and one of the boldest moves I have ever done in an initial encounter. It happened so fast she didn't have a chance to counter.

In her accent, she said, "You're fuckin' smooth, motherfucker," while laughing.

I walked straight out, saying nothing—just glanced back with an expression that said, "Yes, I won." My friends asked as I walked outside if I had got her number. I said, "No, but we will talk again." I could tell they didn't understand and probably had a lot of doubt. Twenty minutes later I got a text that said, "I have to give it to you, that was fucking smooth, well played." I replied, "Hey, desperate times call for desperate measures, and I would not be able to live with myself if I did not give you my best shot."

After that first night meeting Hanna, she and I started talking and texting constantly. We clicked right away because she was spunky, sarcastic, and very quick on her toes. The type of person who, if you give them an inch, will take a shot at your ego, manhood, or whatever else, just for laughs. However, it did not take long for Hanna to come clean and admit that she was in an unhappy marriage.

This was not the first time I made a connection with a married woman. But this was the first time that I was willing to disrespect the sanctity of a couple's union. I had been tempted once, meeting a woman with the booty shape of Serena Williams in the offseason. She was married, and her husband was on a deployment with the military. This woman came on to me at a birthday party, and kissed me in the garage. I had to squeeze her booty right then and there. The temptation was too great. Immediately after kissing and squeezing her, I stopped things from progressing. I said, "Sorry, we should not disrespect your husband and family. I'm just not the type to be entertaining soldier's wives while they are out fighting for my freedom." I know that there is infidelity on both sides; however, I have a little bit of integrity in that regard.

The second married woman who came on to me worked with me in a music group. She was much older than me, and she called me one day saying, "Oh, I'm in your neighborhood, and I made you some brownies." I said, "Okay, cool, stop by, I live at this address..." Just as she arrived, my mother called me on the phone, and as I was talking to my mom I invited her inside. She asked to use the restroom. While I was on the phone with my mom, she walked out of my bathroom with no clothes on. I told my mom I needed to call her back. Then I took a good look at this lady. She did not arouse me, but I did not want to destroy her confidence, so I told her we couldn't do anything because she was married with kids. Well, I guess this example doesn't count because I was not physically attracted to her, so it's not entirely accurate that I honored her relationship.

With Hanna, her beauty and wit overwhelmed me, and I couldn't help abandoning my own rules concerning married women. I asked her why she was willing to entertain another man while married. She said her husband only wanted to play video games and does not cherish her like he used to. Unfortunately, her husband was also active duty military, but my military and deployment clause went out the window. I was whole-heartedly into Hanna. She said she wanted to come to my job and have lunch. At that time, I worked at a federal government facility in the warehouse. Hanna and I were the same age, and neither of us had established our careers; we were both still trying to obtain our college degrees. I was hesitant about her coming to my workplace because a girl like that in a warehouse, hanging around those type of men, would turn them into hounds. Most warehouses are like dog kennels, and Hanna walking through there to meet me was like a cat or side of beef sashaying through the pound. Hanna had a lot of style; she looked good wearing her hair in a lot of different ways, and she wore non-prescription glasses to give herself a scholarly look. Just looking at Hanna you could see the French and Dutch, but with a dancer's physique. Hanna could have easily performed in her own flash dance video like a younger Jenny Lopez.

What I learned quickly is that there needs to be balance when complimenting an extremely beautiful girl. Who wants a person who only ever, and constantly, tells them they are pretty? That gets old quick and makes the recipient feel that their purpose in your life is just to be the beautiful girl. There are also individuals who do not compliment their beautiful mate at all, so it does not go to their head by bolstering their ego. What I have learned is that you do not want a guy or girl at work admiring your partner more than you do. Hanna drove a nice luxury car and seemed to have nice things, but that did not equate to happiness for her. Hanna just wanted the attention of her husband. Usually, I would try to befriend a person like that and keep it platonic, but her personality and beauty were too overwhelming for my better judgment. I was giving Hanna the attention she desired, and we wanted to see more of each other.

One day, Hanna called me and said she was having a New Years' Eve party at her house and that I must come. I said I did not know how it was supposed to work with her husband there, so we ended up devising a shady story. We decided to tell her husband that I was her friend Tonya's cousin from New York. I do not know why we chose New York because I have California-boy written all over my face, speech, and appearance, but we went with it. I told Hanna that I was not coming unless I could bring a friend, which I had to do for safety reasons, and to be an extra set of eyes to read the situation. I selected Jason for a few reasons. Jason is a guy who knows how to talk to any group whether he is versed in the topic or not. He is very popular in San Diego, and there was a good chance he would know someone at the party, or if things went sour he was just a phone call away from bringing in backup. Also, Jason knew how to command the attention of a room and create distractions if I needed alone time with Hanna.

Jason was down to be my wingman, but he doubted the reward was worth the risk. Everyone has their own definition of a dime (10 point) gorgeous woman. Scales and ratings can vary based on taste and experiences. When I woke up on New Years' Eve, I had a dream about being at Hanna's house and seducing her in her bathroom while her husband was in the next room over. I shared that dream with her when I awoke. Hanna and I were nervous about being questioned by her man, but we had some rehearsed answers. Even though I had never been to New York at the time, and could easily be stunned by questions about the city, Hanna believed her husband was not going to interrogate me. Jason and I arrived at Hanna's house late around 11:00 p.m., just an hour before the New Years' count down.

When Hanna answered the door and welcomed us, Jason immediately apologized to me because Hanna was a dime in his eyes too, and the accent made him a believer of the cause. Tonya was no slouch either as Jason had his sights on her as a bonus surprise to the trip. I was surprised to see the type of man she had married. On the surface, he didn't seem to be her equal. He was not garbage, just an average looking black guy. But who knows, maybe he was packing like a horse, and showering her with gifts. Whatever it was, I had confidence that I could get in closer with Hanna if the night went well. I was not surprised to find him playing video games when we shook hands. He had a house of 20 guests, and he was playing games while his wife was hosting in a sexy, white, see-through dinner dress. Jason is a video game head too, but he's a gamer with an MBA, so his diverse conversational abilities were about to come in handy. Jason immediately challenged Hanna's husband to a football video game, and this was perfect for me to advance with Hanna.

Hanna asked me if I wanted a tour of her house and

I said sure. She immediately took me to the bathroom down the hall. There was a candle lit so she didn't bother turning on the light. She guided me into the bathroom and kind of sat up on the sink. Pulling me close to her, she said, "So tell me about that dream again—how were you seducing me in my restroom?" I got excited and nervous at the same time. She was being daring, but her husband was in the next room. Hanna slightly hiked up her dress, and I loved to see the shape of her toned thighs. Her legs were perfect; I could see the definition in her muscles, but they looked smooth and lustrous as buttermilk. I propped myself real close to her and said, "If I could have it my way, I would toss you in the shower and take delight in you like a Dutch apple pie; and trust me, I feel like adding some a la mode to your treat." As soon as things were heating up between us, her husband was walking down the hall, calling out to her to make sure all of the guests had a glass of champagne by 11:50.

Regrettably, we had to join the rest of the party as it was almost time for the countdown. It sucked for me because after the clock rolled around to 12 a.m., and everyone was ready to share the traditional kiss, I had to endure their phony embrace. Jason and I left within an hour. I had seen what I needed to see and had to rethink if this was something that I still wanted to pursue.

I started to give Hanna some space because I can be selfish too and am not always in the mood to share. Some time passed and Hanna called to tell me that she had left her husband. Though it was good news for me, things were still new for her and the separation process was getting nasty for her. She was a full-time student, and the husband had financially cut her off and was not providing any spousal support. But I got a chance to see how strong Hanna was in the process. My primary concern at the time was to emotionally support her because I knew that was in the best interest for her. As time went by, things got easier for her, then she shared how her husband was verbally and somewhat physically abusive. However, Hanna was not a weak woman, and she displayed that she had strength in her, in regard to grinding things out, and making things happen for her on her own. She found a roommate and a car on her own, and she got the chance to keep the family dog, Oliver.

Hanna told me she was ready for me to take her out for real, and I was willing and ready to get us back into the swing of things. It's always amazing to me what a man will do for a woman that he really wants. I am in no way a dog lover, never have been; I was chased too much as a kid by dogs in my neighborhood. That created a barrier for me. Unfortunately, Oliver was a big white dog. I could not tell you what kind of dog, but it was an enormous dog with cotton-like hair, floppy ears, and a big, square black snout. Not the kind of dog that you see often. When I arrived to pick Hanna up for our first official date, I purposely left the flowers I brought for her in the car because I wanted to be a gentleman, but not predictable. Oliver greeted me at the door and I had to return the excitement as if he was my own, just to appease Hanna. But really, I didn't want anyone's animal drooling on my clothes.

Hanna gave me a hard time about not bringing flowers. She said, "I thought you were anticipating our first date, and you couldn't even give me bloody flowers?" I let her go on about it because I knew I had already won. As soon as I opened the car door for her, the flowers and card were sitting in her passenger seat. She looked back at me, and I gestured to her "Zip your lips." Our relationship had a jovial, antagonistic dynamic, and were able to be cynical in a humorous way.

I had reserved a table at this Thai restaurant in La Jolla that I had never been to before. For me, this was risky because I could not attest to the quality of the restaurant or their food, but I wanted to experience something new with Hanna. We enjoyed each other throughout dinner. We had glasses of wine, and the food was delicious. We headed back to her house to enjoy each other's company some more while her roommate was not home, but Oliver sure was playing bodyguard.

We sat on her couch, and the flirting and laughter continued. She suggested that I spend the night because we had too many drinks and it was unsafe to drive home. I told her I'm all for staying over, but I'm not down with sleeping on the couch, and I have to be up early the next morning. Unfortunately, all three of us headed to the bedroom, and I was praying that Oliver would not get to jump in the bed with us because that is where I have to draw the line. Hanna jumped on the bed in a tank top and pajama shorts. Oliver made a move to jump on the bed and she told him no, then showed him to his corner in the room and gave him a bone. We were both a little buzzed and feeling a little loose from the wine, but I held her in high regard and was hesitant to make a move. As she turned the lights off and laid next to me, I said thank you for extending the invitation for me to spend the night, and thinking of my safety. I kissed her on the cheek, then on the neck; and I noticed that she didn't stop me, so I moved my kisses down lower and lower.

Hanna's skin was smooth and silky. I'm not sure if I had ever been with a woman whose skin was so unblemished. I turned her on her stomach because I wanted to kiss her back and squeeze her ass as I kissed it. She just laid there as if I had been hired to give her a massage. I turned her back over and started to kiss her on the inner thigh. I could feel her body tensing up as I moved my lips closer to her pelvis. I took my two fingers and touched the top of her clitoris lightly. Then I kissed her where my fingers had been. Soon after, my kissing turned to licking. As soon as I started to lick her pussy, her hands clenched the sheets. I told her it was ok for her to express herself if she liked what I was doing. "Are you bloody mad?" she said. "Don't stop I like it" she said, pushing my head back down between her legs. I could taste her arousal, and I wanted more of her crème brulee.

The deeper my tongue went, the softer and warmer the taste became. Hanna's vagina was very wet as I alternated my tongue and fingers inside of her. She began moaning so loudly that Oliver sat up, and we had to call him off and let him know things were more than fine. I sat up and was ready to do some drilling with my principal instrument. I was above her just about to take my dip, and Hanna stopped me, saying she just wasn't ready. As an adult, I have never been the type of man to negotiate sex while in the moment. Sure, when I was a kid and sex was new, I often had some sort of speech or a rebuttal prepared for various situations. But in this case I knew that Hanna had not been with a man other than her husband in years so uncertainty may surface. I did not push the issue, and we went to sleep without completing.

The week after, we continued to talk, and I even met her at the dog park. That was my first time going to a dog park. It was cool to see different types of dogs and owners bonding. One thing I noticed about Hanna, which was a turn-off, was that every time we went out it was on my dime, and after a while I felt there was no equal contribution. Hanna was gorgeous, and she knew it; our chemistry was legit, and I believe she knew that as well. Hanna joined me one evening when I was playing piano at an upscale restaurant for a local band. She even hung out with my coworkers during occasional happy hours. She was the type of girl who could fit in with any social crowd because she was smart and confident. However, I started to feel like I did not have her full attention.

Beautiful girls are always going to get attention. So for average guys to match up, it takes constant work until the girl is yours. I was not able to make Hanna mine, and this was the first time as an adult that I was not able to close the deal or overcome the inferior complex that can show up when you're not the best looking one in the couple. I made it to Hanna's bed, but I failed to make it to her head and heart. When a person has a hot commodity within reach, there is a hidden clock with a second hand ticking away. Time is of the essence, and I dropped the ball with Hanna. But then again, Hanna showed no personal investment such as opening her wallet or heart during our escapade, so maybe the deal was never mine to close. I may have just been the bridge Hanna was traveling from her long-term relationship back into the dating scene.

-VI-

Good Loving, Bad Timing, Equals Unfinished

I had a previous job delivering supplies to different clinics within the same medical facilities. Being a delivery man is cool because you have daily encounters with multiple people and sometimes relationships are built. Although, like many jobs, people judge others based on their occupation, and the treatment an individual may receive is centered around their job title. When I worked for FedEx, I did deliveries at an upscale mall. In most cases, the front desk girl had her nose in the air, even though she only worked the register for Tiffany Jeweler or Neiman Marcus. During a standard delivery, I would barely get eye contact. But on payday Friday, when I was delivering the overnight checks, I would receive a "Thank you," and "We appreciate your services, sir." Personally, I did not like being treated like a delivery boy because I knew it was the "temporary me" while in college. I knew my dreams and talents would offer more than delivering boxes to a home or business on schedule.

One day, I was delivering supplies to a routine clinic on my route, and my usual point of contact, Odell, was not in his office that day. I decided to try the room next door because it was part of the same clinic. I looked on the door plate, and it read Miss Rachel Walker. I said, "Excuse me, are you able to sign for a package for me? It is for this department." Her reply was, "Is this protocol? You don't have a second delivery attempt or third until you get the right person?" I laughed as soon as she said that. *She must be kidding, right?* Rachel had a spunky attitude like Punky Brewster. I finally said to her, "I would appreciate if you can do me this one favor and sign for the packages, Ma'am, so I can be on my way," In a sarcastic tone, Rachel said, "Let this be the last time—now be gone!" I knew she was kidding, but I had the urge to show her that I was not just the facility delivery boy.

Rachel was attractive, and we were both in our mid to late 20's at the time. Rachel had a white complexion and a loud personality. I noticed from a photo in her office that she had a daughter, and the child was mixed with possibly black and white, and I did not see a ring on her finger. (It is amazing to me how you can look at a person's desk and tell so much about them based on the pictures in the office and the way the room is set up.) As soon as I got back to my work desk, I located Rachel's email address in the network, and I emailed her to thank her for being a team player. If a woman wants to play the sarcasm game, I am all for it; I stay sharp on my toes. I had to tell Rachel immediately, please don't make the mistake of just viewing me as the delivery guy; I have more to offer than just office supplies. "Oh, please," she said. "I am not interested in whatever line you're trying to use on me." I said, "Hey, forget it, I was just being friendly, not trying to put the cyber moves on you." Time passed after that initial email correspondence, and I had many more deliveries with her department, and more exchanges with her. However, I did not show too much interest, but we did share some laughs during brief exchanges. After a while, her initial perceptions of me began to change. We exchanged numbers, and Rachel started to invite me out around her friends; but she never showed more than friendship intentions towards me.

I became fond of Rachel because she reminded me of my sister—a single parent of two who was trying her best to move up in her career. Rachel had a very diverse group of friends; some of her girls were African-American, Caribbean, Hispanic, and Rachel, of course, was pure Caucasian. Out of all of her friends, Rachel was the loud-mouth—the girl who will cause a scene, and call anyone out on their bullshit and lies. However, there was another side of Rachel that was about motherhood, career, education, spiritual peace, and relaxation. The first time I hung out with Rachel and her friends was at an outdoor barbecue. I did not bring a wingman with me, and I only stayed for a few hours so her friends and I could get a feel for each other.

The next time I hung out with Rachel and her friends was downtown at a club. We all went out dancing, and this time I brought my friend Lawrence. He was a good wingman because he knew how to make girls laugh, he liked to dance, and he could operate independently in a social setting. Meaning, sometimes if a group of friends becomes detached from each other in a social setting, each may become less extroverted, and their confidence diminishes because they lack the power in numbers. I have always believed if you are trying to make a move on a girl you will have better success if she is alone because friends will give the girl the advantage in a conversation. Friends can make the individual less vulnerable and create a stage to perform, versus an honest flowing conversation. Lawrence did think that Rachel was cute, but it was evident to him that she was loud and needed some taming. It was hard for me to figure out Rachel because she would invite me out but not treat me as her guest.

When we were out at the club with her friends, one of her friends was giving me more attention than she was, and this was the second time this had happened. I started to believe that Rachel was not that into me. I danced with her friend Kristy, who was a nice looking black girl with curly hair and a voluptuous round butt. Kristy was flirting with me, but I kept looking around for Rachel, and eventually spotted her dancing with other people. I guess she could not help it if she attracts the attention of others. Kristy could tell that I was more concerned about Rachel than our dance, and that is when the dancing intensified and she kissed me on my lips. Yes, it was a sweet, soft kiss that I did enjoy, but I did not initiate the kiss. Kristy was feeling me and giving me the attention that I wished Rachel would have provided to me. I felt like if I stayed at the club much longer things would have turned out to be detrimental to my chances with Rachel. The next day I did come clean to Rachel. I said, "Hey, your girl was on me hard last night, and she kissed me. But, for the record, I am not into her. I'm only interested in your attention." Rachel was immediately upset with me, and her anger stage helped me to understand and pinpoint her hesitation in getting involved with me altogether.

Rachel was like all girls who have been hurt or disappointed by a particular group of men. Rachel's preference as a Caucasian female is to date African American men. Interracial dating is common, but those who do still encounter a lot of criticism in society. I do not think that there is anything wrong with having a preference in who you choose to date. We have preferences on what color car we want, what type of neighborhood we want to live in, and what kind of food we want to limit to our daily diet. Having a preference or stereotyping are two different things, but we all do it—yes, all of us. Like many others, I stereotype on a smaller scale all of the time. If I am in a rush, needing to checkout groceries in a store, and I see two clerks open—one is a young, college-age male, the other is an older, heavyset lady, I am going to subconsciously (or consciously) choose the younger man. Because I determine, based on appearance alone, that this person is going to get me through the transaction the quickest. Sometimes people associate fat people with slow and lazy tendencies, which isn't always the case, but, without thinking, those baked-in societal notions tend to sway our thinking.

In college math class if you are stuck on a problem and you have an Asian-American classmate to the left and an African American classmate to your right, most people are going to turn to their left and ask the Asian-American classmate the math question for tips. Now, take those same classmates outdoors and create a team for a sports game and you will be more inclined to take the African American as your teammate. Unfortunately, we still live in a society that judges books by their covers. Excluding a race, or forecasting failure on a race of people to complete a task, function, job, or ability based on their skin tone is wrong. Yes, certain cultures embrace different activities and tasks more than others. Those cultures may also be known to dominate that field. But even with the historical data to support our stereotypes, it is wrong to put limitations on race or skin complexion, and we should gauge individuals on a case-by-case basis.

It is especially evident that this is still happening in our society when Marshall Mathers, AKA Eminem, the hip-hop rapper, debuted in the music industry with headlines all touting a white man as the best Rapper in Rap (black music). Did people overlook his skill to rhyme and compose thoughtful lyrics, and crown him king just because of the color of his skin? In the 2016 Olympics, Simone Manuel made history as the first black woman to win gold in an individual swimming event. Simone Biles dominated the Women's Gymnastics like the world has never seen before. Michelle Carter's case is different because people did not discount her due to race but due to her size as she prevailed as a gold medalist in the shot put. Claressa Shields was one of my favorite stories, as she was discounted by the media and sports community due to her socio-economic disadvantage and upbringing. This sort of treatment ranges from Eminem (Grammy award winning Rap musician) to the Williams sisters (professional tennis champions), to Sofia Vergara (Emmy award winning & pop culture icon), Gloria Estefan (Latin American music icon), and Mary Barra (First female CEO of a major automaker, GM). All the names mentioned above, and many more, have broken down barriers, due to race, sex, age, culture, and societal stereotypes. By removing stereotypes, we expand the opportunity for greatness to happen, and minimize being surprised by a person's achievement, acknowledging them simply because they are great at what they do.

In the dating world, after you have some bad experiences with a particular type of man or woman, we start to categorize instead of letting each situation stand alone. Rachel had some bad experiences with the two former black men that she had dated. She had even experienced a divorce with the father of her children. However, just because I am black, I am not interested in having to prove the difference between myself and other black men. There has been some widely disseminated wrong and adverse information concerning black males. Rachel did not know that her problem was not black males; it was the type of men, and the pool from which she was selecting them. Yes, there is a group of guys who are lazy, and would rather play video games than work. There is also a demographic of young men who are still chasing their professional sports dream at the local YMCA at age 29 instead of providing for their home. These situations are not exclusive to black males; these conditions connect to the men's age, socio-economic upbringing, and maturity.

Instead of judging by their skin color, pull the thread on the individual and see what example was given to them to be a man. In my other book "From Father to Daddy" I cover the topic of how men need to see the example more than just hear about how to lead the household. Doing some information gathering will reveal if this is the man or woman that you desire. For black women to say, "I want a white man or nonminority male because they have better credit, and/or more career ambition," is stinking thinking. Equally wrong is when a white female says, "I want to date a black male because they are better sex partners, or "I want a Latino partner because they are more romantic." Black men have been catching a bad reputation for years for reaching success and deciding to have a non-black woman on their arm to enjoy this new, better life. Many accuse black men of thinking that a white woman on your arm makes you feel more satisfied or accomplished. For a black man to want to mate with a non-black female for the sake of the skin complexion or hair grain or texture is wrong. That is not a preference; that is racism because you are making one group or race superior to the other.

Black women receive labels as angry and more combative than other cultures/races. These labels are stereotypes that are unfair and lack honest examination. People are like fruit, and the foundation of the tree down to the root can determine the condition of that fruit. Every person comes from an upbringing experience that shaped them into the person they are today. Black women have received an unfair shake, and a late invitation to the party called self-confidence and success. Look at the newsstand magazines; the celebration of black women compared to white women is a far disparity. Thank God for Essence magazine, Ebony, and Vibe who make it a point to highlight African American women's beauty and contribution to fashion, business, societal issues, and pop culture. In the last decade Vanity Fair Magazine cover has been graced by only four black women: Beyoncé Knowles, Rihanna, Viola Davis, and Kerry Washington. However, there have been many more beautiful and fruitful black ladies that deserve a celebration. Yes, there are tons of black women who warranted a cover page before Bruce/Caitlyn Jenner.

I am in no way accusing Vanity of being partial to a particular skin tone or race of women, but they are negligent in not having balance in who they choose to grace the cover. Many black women are successful today, and their futures are bright, but I encourage people to stop assuming. Take a moment and ask the person's story. I honestly believe there are a group of women who are not mad and angry, but are just tired of the games and not being considered equal, which demeans their value. More dialogue needs to happen between the African-American dating group to get a better understanding on why we are not choosing each other to love. People who are not the same race may not understand the life challenges and stereotypes that their opposite sex is experiencing.

Also, if you have a mate who has been misused or damaged by someone who was similar to yourself, you have to reject and disprove those projections. Getting involved with someone who has experienced sexual abuse requires far more patience, empathy, and gentleness. Rachel needed me to disprove her assumptions of black men. Even though her friend and I kissed, I was not trying to hide what happened. Instead, I was forthcoming, and told her that this was the attention I needed from her. Rachel decided to give me a chance and asked me to meet her at this bar to watch Monday night football. This time she was bringing only one friend, and I brought Lawrence as my friend distractor. Rachel was a huge Broncos fan and loved to talk crap until she could get under your skin. During the game, we played a game of pool.

Playing pool with someone I like makes the game five times better for me. The game of pool, for guys, is also perfect for sexual innuendos, which is what I did all night. Rachel and I were finally flirting one-on-one while tuning out the entire room all night long. Just before I made the winning shot on the 8-ball, I told her to stand next to the pocket where I was going to shoot the ball inside. I wanted her to crouch over the hole. She doubted my skills and I asked her, "How do you want it, nice and hard, or gentle and light? Rachel, you seem like the hair-pulling type, so I'm just going to jam it in there," and that's when I smashed the 8-ball right into the hole. She was stunned as she felt the ball vibrate while leaning on the pool table. We laughed and hugged it out, and she gave me a kiss on the cheek in good sportsmanship. She then asked me to try this steak, and I said, "Here, at this bar?" "No way, steak and pool tables do not mix." She told me to trust her judgment. I did, and surprisingly, we had a great juicy steak with mashed potatoes at a sketchy sports bar. *Wow, I was sure wrong about prejudging this establishment.*

Rachel and I were starting to build a strong rapport. What I knew about Rachel was that she was independent, smart, loved her kids, and believed in working hard and playing just as hard. Though she still made it difficult for me to get one-on-one time on a consistent basis. She was the type of girl who would cancel the day before if I did advanced planning, so I was better off being spontaneous or waiting for her to make a move. My birthday was coming up, and I made reservations for us to go out, dress up, and play the romantic part. My birthday is the same week of Halloween, and she invited me out downtown with her and her friends to hang out. This night was a work night, and two days before our planned birthday date, Lawrence and I met up with her friends at a club in downtown San Diego. After the club, Rachel wanted to go to a haunted house. Lawrence and I were not in the mood for that, but we waited around because they wanted to take us to a place called Double Deuces. I had never been to Double Deuces or heard of it, but I was in for an entertaining night.

Our group was large. There were about 12 of us, and inside of Double Deuces was discounted alcohol and a mechanical bull ride. The bull ride operator thought he was so slick because when he had a girl with a skirt or low cut shirt on the bull, he made sure that things were jiggling in the right places. I could tell the operator's primary goal was for ladies to fall with their goodies exposed. I got on the bull and was bounced around like a drunk ragdoll. Rachel pulled me outside to the club's patio while everyone was taking turns bull riding. Once we made it outside, I started to tell her again that I was into her and what is the holdup? In the middle of my speech, she told me to just shut up and kiss her. She then pulled me in to kiss her, and it was the best kiss of my child and adult life combined. I used to take pride in my kisses as a teenager. I used to play all the stupid games like tie the stem of a cherry in a knot with my tongue, somehow proving to a group that I was a good kisser. I have had some bad kisses, and great kisses, like everyone has, but by far, Rachel Walker was the best kisser I ever encountered. She had the perfect balance of tongue and lips. I had to sober up for a good two minutes to comprehend how great of a kisser she was. Unfortunately for me, the patio kiss is where Rachel wanted to leave the action at for the night. The night was late, everyone was drunk and had to work in the morning.

The next day I reached out to Rachel, and there was no response. I just wanted to follow up on our fun night and make sure things were on the upbeat. My big date that I had been planning for my birthday was the next day, and I was uneasy about the chance of her backing out. Needless to say, Rachel canceled the day of because she was very ill from the alcohol and was admitted to the hospital. Of course, my primary concern was her health, but I still felt unlucky. Rachel did apologize for not being able to go out on my birthday, and surprisingly she invited me on a trip to Big Bear to bring in the New Year with her friends and family. I did not know what to expect because this was an overnight trip for two nights. I accepted the invite and met her up in Big Bear. I received a warm reception, but unfortunately for me, Rachel had a lady friend in the mountains that made it difficult for Rachel and I to have some alone time. It was cramped because it was four families, four bedrooms, and two solo acts.

Rachel got upset with me because I wanted to watch an NBA game during some down time. We had a petty argument over this, and it rubbed us both the wrong way. While in the mountains, I did not have phone reception or access to the internet for 48 hours. Nor was Rachel giving me a great share of attention, and absolutely no affection. Rachel was upset because she felt that on a mountain trip like this, I should always be available to group fun and interaction. All I wanted to do is catch one Lakers game, (and this was during their glory years with Kobe and Gasol). At the end of the trip, I felt like I was still in the audition period for Rachel to see if she should consider us as an option.

I have kissed and had solid friendships with white females, but never got to the point where I was thinking of being an exclusive couple. Not for any particular reason, just as an adult, I take commitment more seriously. But Rachel was a keeper in my eyes. Yes, there were some rough edges and baggage to overcome, but I felt my baggage could complement hers in some way. And I knew she needed someone with patience because she was tired of being duped by men, particularly black men.

Rachel was a leader in social and professional settings. She did not bite her tongue, but I was prepared to be the one who kept her calm until she needed to sink her teeth into someone. Even though Rachel and I could not say that Big Bear was an ideal connection for either of us, she final granted me my one-on-one date after five months of hit-and-miss misfortune. I made reservations at a lovely restaurant on the water in Del Mar, California. I had dined at this place once years ago, and I remembered it was a romantic and lively place with a good seafood cioppino dish. Rachel met me at my condo and jumped into my SUV. We headed to the restaurant. I was so relieved at the beginning of the date because we finally made it to a date without a cancellation on her end. Rachel looked splendid in a black strapless dress; her hair was up, and I could tell she'd done a few leg extensions in the gym that week because her legs were picture perfect. Normally, she was in business casual or party attire. Nothing had ever said, "I want you to want me" until this night. I was happy to find out that she had never been to or heard of the restaurant that I had chosen, so that was a plus for me.

We had a candlelight setting on the water with delicious food and wine. We finally connected, and I got her to let her guard down for the evening. After dinner, we stopped at a wine bar to grab a bottle for home. Ok, I am big on not judging a book by its cover, but it was a pleasant surprise that Rachel was into soul music and R&B. One of her favorite artists was Musiq Soulchild. I usually do not use my music talents to get ahead with a girl. Yes, in high school, it was fun to have the girls gather around me in the theater while I played K-Ci & JoJo on the piano. I know many acoustic guitar players love to profess their love through their instruments; however, I always preferred just to speak and use my words. When Rachel and I arrived at my house, I took her into my music room and poured her a glass of wine. I told her to stand up, and I walked her over to my Fender Rhodes piano that sits about three and a half feet off the ground. I made her put her hands on the piano keys. I walked up behind her and put my arms on either side of her like we were one body. I told her to put her hands atop mine while I played her a song. She smiled, and said this was new for her. I started playing "Teach Me How to Love" by Musiq Soulchild, and as I played, she became happy. I was not playing as smooth because I was a little buzzed from the alcohol, but it had the same effect and results.

She turned around and started kissing me, and I was thinking here we go again, *the girl with the magical motion tongue and soft lips.* We moved into my bedroom, kissing on the bed; then suddenly, I start thinking about how much I like her, and I end up more focused on being her man than being her lover for the night. I was thinking so hard in that moment that I thought myself out of an erection. Rachel was ready to go, aroused and all, but I could not get the car out of the garage. She even offered to wax it with her tongue, but my mind was stuck somewhere else. Then she says, "Come on, it's good—you just gotta get in it." I laughed because that was an arrogant statement, but I loved the confidence. Needless to say, Rachel decided to go home. The non-performance was all my error, but I wasn't embarrassed. I think Rachel got the upper hand in that relationship because everything was happening on her terms, and once again, I wanted her heart not just a piece of her pie.

For months, Rachel and I laughed about the incident, but failure for me to seal the deal caused more separation between us. We both started to see other people. We remained friends and respectful, but we both knew we had some unfinished business. Over a year passed because our timing had been off. And by then, we both were in committed relationships. But when we came across each other again, we knew that if we were on the market, we would have been an item. Being in a situation like that is weird because I was in a relationship with someone else but I could see my potential with Rachel, and vice versa for her. Finally, the committed relationship I was in had run its course. I emailed Rachel out of the blue, and she said my timing was strange because she had just been talking to her dad about me. I asked about what? She said that she had admitted to her dad that I might have been the solid guy she had been looking for all this time.

I said, "Well, if you're admitting that I'm a good catch for you then why are we still playing these cat and mouse games? There has to be something about me that makes you unsure or insecure? Please be honest—I have thick skin, and you already hold our awkward night over my head." Rachel said that I may be too nice, and may not have the type of personality that can control a woman like her. Though she was not looking to be controlled, she clarified, just for a strong-willed equal. Yes, no woman wants to be bossed around but they do want a man who is capable of leading with authority and guiding with a confident, loving hand. Truth be told, I am a nice guy on the surface, but can also be a jerk who has high, but reasonable, expectations. Perhaps Rachel was mistaking my kindness and desire to be with her for weakness? At that time, I was not ready to pursue her like times before because it had always led to a dead end. So I told her that if she wanted to go out she needed to plan the date because my days of relentless chasing were over. Rachel thought about it, and told me to pick her up Friday night at her house.

When I arrived at her house she was wearing tight pants and a cute top. She gave me a short tour around the house, then I jumped in her car to enjoy whatever she had planned for us. We went to an indoor car racing warehouse where we raced in a group. It was very competitive, and once again the trash-talking began. This time the result was different, though, Rachel clipped me on the final lap because some stupid driver cut me off. It was good that she won because I was able to extend the same sportsmanship that she had when I was the victor in our game of pool. I normally do not like to lose any game, especially those I play against women and children. However, she liked that I gave her props. After the race, Rachel took me to a Reggae and hip-hop underground club. At the underground club, things got heated in a good way. I'm not a dancer, but she served me enough drinks to where I was good enough for a two-step rhythm.

"Come on, let's dance," Rachel said.

"I'm forbidden to dance when I'm in this condition," I said.

"Why?"

"Because my hands and pelvis do not know how to behave."

"I think you're scared."

"No, I'm scared for you because there are some pretty solid dancers in this club, and I'm not convinced that you can keep up."

"Oh, so you doubt my skills because I'm white!?"

"I doubt your skills because you're a soccer mom. You belong on the field, or on the sidelines handing out water, not on the dance floor."

"Put your drink down and get your ass over here."

"If I come can I touch? But if I touch I might want to taste."

"Taste what?"

"Your strawberry shortcake. Sure, you don't have red hair, but you have cute freckles and a sweet tongue."

"First I need to see if you can hang on the dance floor."

We started to dance, and Rachel and I began to sweat. The room was full, and we had no option but to dance close. Rachel put her arms around my neck, and we were flirting. When a hip-hop song was played by the DJ, she turned around and started to put it on me. Honestly, I couldn't hang, and I just had to hold on for the ride. And, if you do, please stop thinking that white girls can't dance because Rachel was moving her body like a snake to the point where I thought she was auditioning for the T.V. show "So You Think You Can Dance?" Her rhythm was perfect, and the positive friction between us was even better. The DJ started playing slow jams, and I grabbed her and started kissing her; my hands were rubbing on her ass. We did not care who else was in the room; we finally had each other in a happy and fulfilling place. We danced and kissed for over an hour. We left the club sweaty and went back to her house.

When we got back to her house, she opened up the garage, and I saw her pool table. I immediately grabbed her hand and walked her up to the table and said, "Remember when I spanked you in pool? I really wanted to punish you in other ways." I started to kiss her and undo her pants; I wanted redemption. Yes, the laughing at my expense was cute, but not an accurate reflection of my sexual ambition. I pulled her pants off and turned her back to me as she leaned over the rail of the pool table. I moved her hair to the side so I could kiss her neck and gradually placed my kisses down her back to her butt. Rachel was just letting me do whatever I felt. As I caressed the side of her hips, my tongue licked the top of her butt crack, and her body started responding to every touch. I spun around and lifted her up to the edge of the pool table. I told her I admired her and asked if it was okay for me to express that admiration. She bit her bottom lip and shook her head yes in anticipation. I grabbed her legs and spread them open, then kissed her calf, her thigh, and finally made it down to her sweet strawberry shortcake.

"I'm going to write my name in your filling with my tongue," I said, moving in.

She palmed my forehead and said, "Hey, don't start

anything if you don't know how to finish it."

"Are you suggesting because I am black that I do not know how to perform oral sex?" I said.

She giggled.

"You surprised me on the dance floor, grant me the courtesy to return the amazement."

I commenced dining on her cake with the goal of reaching the strawberry cream filling in the middle. I used my tongue, my fingers, and my lips to pleasure her. There is this technique that I like to use when I'm fully in the moment with my lover. I put my two middle fingers with the palm of my hand facing up; as my fingers were penetrating Rachel, I placed my chin in the palm of my hand while I licked and sucked on her clitoris. To make this more pleasurable, you can't just be wild and random. Just like a guy does not want another person going uncontrollably wild on their genitals, it's the same concept for women. Finding the right pressure and motions are vital. As I licked and lightly stroked my fingers inside Rachel, I found a rhythm that she was reacting to consistently. I used my ears to listen and my hands to feel the vibration of her body, and let her body tell me when to go harder and faster. Her pussy was leaking all over my chin like a popsicle melting in my mouth. I knew it was getting good, but I did not want her to orgasm yet. Selfishly, I was saving that for my dick. I was not sure if Rachel was a multiple orgasm type of girl or if she was a one and done. At that point, my cock was so aroused that I had pre-ejaculation in my underwear. Rachel thought I was so sweet, and I had that in the forefront of my mind.

Yes, the natural thing would be to jump on the pool

table and start working her, but I'm never eager to be on a hard surface with bare knees. Sorry, I stay within my limits. Rachel stood up and pulled my penis out, then reached further down in my underwear and cupped my balls in her hands, like the dirty Jennifer Aniston character in the movie *Horrible Bosses*. She said, "Are you ready to give this to me?" I immediately turned her back to me and elevated one leg onto the pool table. I have no problem being firm with a girl in a sexual scenario. I'm just not going to choke a female during sex until she is about to pass-out. I do not care how much of a rush and joy that is; for me, it's too risky, and I'm too scared for the worst to occur. But I had Rachel from behind, and we were in her garage on her pool table. I was stroking her deep from the back. She started to establish a tempo and the sex was getting louder and faster.

I got a handful of her hair, and I yanked it back so hard that it forced her to chin up. She said, "Oh shit!" I said, "Yeah, this shit is mine tonight." I slapped her ass hard and the sound echoed and resonated vociferously because we were in a room with a concrete floor and empty walls. She said, "Keep going, you're going to make me cum." I said, "Go ahead and bust, but save another round for me." As Rachel started to cum, she began to bite and moan on the strap of her shirt. (My guess was she wanted to be mindful of her neighbors.) Her vagina was super juicy and throbbing on my penis. Rachel turned me around and placed my butt against the edge of the pool table. As I leaned against the edge of the table, she fucked me as she leaned over to grab her ankles, bouncing on top of me. Her back was arched all the way down, and she had a smooth bouncing motion while I had my hands on her hips from behind.

I felt like we were back at the reggae hip-hop club, and I could barely hang again because she was giving it all to me. She told me, "You know you want to release—you can't handle this," She was talking crap, but she was right; I couldn't hold it in any longer. I warned her that I was about to cum, and I took my dick out and ejaculated down her back. It squirted uncontrollably, and it even got in her hair. She instantly snapped out of the sexual mood and said, "Damn, you got your shit in my hair." In a snarky tone, I said, "Oh, sorry—nice guys aren't supposed to behave in that way." We both laughed as she called me a prick.

After that enjoyable evening, I was sort of expecting our relationship to launch, but it did not. Rachel consumed her time with being a mom, and when she had spare time she was not looking for it to be exclusive to me. However, I had my side distractions, and I was more inclined to the women who wanted my attention. We seemed to keep getting involved with other people, then we'd come back to the table for a progress report to see if it was time for us to be an item. I think we both enjoyed the friendship as much as the romance, but for me, this is when a pair should strike. I do not believe that Rachel had ever coupled with a man who had done his part as a provider, protector, and leader. Rachel's independence was not making room for me, but most importantly, she did not trust that I could be the man for her. Rachel was a leader in her home and with her children. Rachel was familiar with being the bread winner and the one with the ambition and aspiration in a relationship. Rachel was God-fearing and compassionate. Many women think that all the good men are taken, and that is why they try to sleep with a married man. The truth is Rachel could not get out of her own way, and the moment she did I was not available, or it was bad timing. Maybe I was blinded by my own self-confidence and could not see the part that prevented Rachel from fully engaging with me.

Rachel and I went through a cooling off period, then we happened to run into each other at a mutual friend's Halloween party. Once again, we danced, flirted, and kissed. Everything felt right when we were together, but when I was out of her sight, I was out of her mind. I loved Rachel, and the crazy thing was, she never gave me a reason to love her. I guess I was in love with the potential joy and completeness that we could bring to each other's life. It was our working lives that brought us together, and the intellectual and witty cat and mouse chase that kept us coming back for more. Our timing was poor and never convenient. Our love connection never got to blossom because choosing each other was never the priority. Rachel will always be the girl I think back on and say to myself, "What if?"

-VII-

You Intimidate Me and I love It

It was January 1st, and I was looking for a change. I had brought the New Year in alone for the first time in a while. No one to hold, love, laugh or play with. One thing that I need in life is female interaction, even if it is just playful banter, but I found myself feeling incomplete because I was unable to get the girl I wanted in Rachel. At that time, I was in and out of another relationship with a woman named Nicole. I needed to change my dating pool. There is a small percentage of people who date individuals from their same place of employment. There are others who find mates through social events, mutual friends, or academic classes, but rarely do you run into Mr. or Mrs. Right in the produce aisle at the market. However, what *has* been growing in popularity in recent years are dating and matchmaking websites. I even know of a few success stories shared with me by close family members. When I was a young adult, I thought online dating was silly, potentially dangerous, desperate, and lazy. Well, it turns out that is more efficient if you know how to vet profiles properly. But still.

I made the decision to do a free 30-day trial with a dating website to see if it was something that could change my normal dating experiences. There are obvious pros and cons to online matching and dating. The pros are that it is like reviewing a resume, and you can see and request clear information before having an in-person exchange. The con is people lie (harsh truth), to embellish their "resume," and attract the job or individual they're seeking. When a man wants someone, he will disguise himself to be what the girl wants until he gets her. I always thought a person's true colors are not revealed until you disappoint them or make them upset. When a buddy tells me that he has been seeing this new girl and things are just perfect, I always ask have you made her angry yet? How did she respond? From my experience, in the first phase of a relationship, people can stay in character for up to 90 days, then you meet their real side.

With online dating, it's important to be aware of the tricks you may come across. People put up pictures of their cute friends. Girls take headshots to avoid showing their muffin-top waist. Guys take pictures in front of their friend's luxury SUV. It can all be amusing—girls trying to attract others by using sex appeal, and men drawing their prey in by using material things. Both genders are guilty of using pictures that are three (or more) years old. Guys use pictures while they were in military-service shape and women use pictures from before the baby. Not everyone is trying to scheme and scam, but asking the right questions and paying attention to what is being typed—the grammar and the content, can help weed out the inconsistencies in a person's story. A guy's purpose can be sniffed out early if you just pay attention to the language during the exchange. Is he anxious to see you? Is he requesting to exchange personal contact information so he can get personal pictures sent to his phone? Is he commenting on your intellect and other personal interests that are listed, or just the profile picture? Guys, however, are not the only ones champing at the bit to see the physical features of the person on the other end of the internet line. Personally, I was honest in my profile about my income, my education, my baggage, and appearance. I posted a picture of myself with short hair and no hair. A picture with a full beard, and one with a clean goatee. No, I didn't have six-pack-abs, but I looked good in my clothes.

My advantage was my texting dialogue. In that first free 30-day trial I had fun, just meeting and weeding people out. The cool thing about this dating site was that you could see who viewed your profile page, but it can be disappointing when someone you might like sees your page and does not leave a note. When someone viewed my page, I saw it as a good thing, because they thought I was attractive for a moment, so there may be hope for me to capitalize on that down the road. I did not come across anyone I was ready to meet in-person until I ran across the profile of Sharmaine Lewis; her profile inspired me to call her "Miss Unbelievable." Not just because she was incredibly cute in her photos, but because of the things she was doing. What I got from Sharmaine's profile picture was that she was a young, black female who rode motorcycles (the street bike type)—pink and black leather biker suit and all.

Sharmaine loved to ski, travel, and play football with contact gear. The dating site showed that we were both checking out each other's pages for a few days, so I finally reached out to her. I was not trying to be too smooth; I just wanted to gauge her level of interest, and possibly get on the phone with her.

After small computer messaging conversations, I got her to agree to meet me for lunch because we were both living in San Diego County. We were both going with the flow and not trying to force anything, but when things go good it is natural to want more and I wanted some face time. After agreeing to meet me for lunch, the next morning she had buyer's remorse and said this was a mistake and sorry for wasting my time. When I received that message I was immediately in recapture mode. I knew that Sharmaine and I had developed a connection messaging each other for the previous week or so, and I wasn't going to let her nerves ruin it for both of us. When it comes to online dates, most people are serious about making a connection that is genuine with the possibility of it becoming long-term. No, I was not thinking long-term with Sharmaine so soon, but I did not give her a reason to want to back off.

I messaged Sharmaine and told her that I wanted her to feel comfortable, but also felt that we needed to follow through with meeting up, and not sell this opportunity short. I was not prepared to guarantee that it would be love or a perfect match, but I definitely knew that we would have an enjoyable lunch. Sharmaine quickly changed her mind, and sent me her mobile number, so I could text her the details of the meetup. I was not sure if I wanted to call her just to hear her voice and confirm that she was real, but I like taking risks, so I gambled and decided not to call her. I'd wait to hear her voice face to face. The next Saturday, I asked her to meet me for brunch at a restaurant called The Fig Tree. She was running a little late, so we ended up meeting at 11 a.m. I was slightly nervous because there is always the fear factor, wondering *are we going to be physically attracted to each other?* She seemed very accomplished, and I hoped my self-confidence could sustain throughout the conversation.

Finally, the waitress escorts Sharmaine to my table where I was awaiting her arrival. She was flowing in her strut in every way possible. Her silky black her was flat-ironed past her shoulders. She was petite with slim hips, curves, a pleasant smile, and current with her fashion. Before she even said hello, I felt like Ice Cube, and I knew that today was going to be a good day. I stood up as she approached the table because I knew I was in the presence of royalty. As we engaged in conversation I felt more comfortable than I did behind the computer. She felt like an old friend, but some of that sense of connection was likely influenced by the fact that we were both around the same age and from southern California. She was very intelligent and proper but was still a woman who could get urban if she needed too. I discovered that Sharmaine was a nurse manager, property owner, and considering pursuing her doctorate in nursing or nurse anesthetist school in her near future. She was not even 30 years old yet, but was a leader in her career field, and an independent female in upscale San Diego.

Surprisingly, I also learned that Sharmaine was a wide receiver for a professional female football team and did multiple social activities. It was very difficult for my achievements to stack up against hers. Hearing her stories and the goals for her life was intimidating, but I loved it. I grew up around women who were highly educated and ambitious. My mother was the bread-winner in our household, but that did not wavier my father's confidence or position of authority. I reflected back to my adolescent experience with Janina and how her early success diminished my confidence. I was not going to let that happen again; I knew professionally, I was not on the same level as Sharmaine, but I was confident that I was on the right path and my ambition could match hers.

Sharmaine and I had a three to four-hour brunch. We laughed, joked, and flirted at the table. I believe in showing my true self, and letting the person make an honest decision if they want a second date. As we wrapped things up, we both felt like we wanted more time because the connection was so authentic and refreshing. I had to play at an event at 7 p.m. that Saturday evening, so I had to disconnect and prepare for that engagement. I sent her a text saying, "Why do I feel the urge to ask you to a movie tonight? Is that weird to want my first two dates with you on the same day?" Her response was, "Let's do it!" I smiled from ear to ear, and as soon as I played my last note, I called her with instructions to meet me at a theater near her house for the late night showing. This time she was waiting for me on the steps of the movie theater where she had already purchased the tickets. Her initiative to grab the tickets, knowing I was behind on time, was a big sign to me that I had found someone who knows how to flow with me and work as a team.

We enjoyed the movie, but more importantly, we enjoyed the opening connection we had found in each other.

Secretly we were both surprised that we got lucky enough to find someone who we both could not wait to get to the second date with and beyond. Sharmaine was a busy person who frequently traveled for her job and personal interests. However, we both preferred to book and plan our next date ahead of time. Early in the relationship, we went to a Thai restaurant for lunch, then frozen yogurt. As we were leaving the frozen yogurt place, a homeless man asked us for some spare change. She looked straight at me. Then the homeless man looked at me with expectation in his eyes. I was confused by her putting the pressure on me. I gave the guy a couple of dollars, then I asked Sharmaine if she was testing my generosity or charity. She responded, no. Sharmaine said she does not give to homeless people anymore because the last homeless guy called her a Bitch. I laughed as soon as she told me and said, "So you are punishing all the other destitute people because of one bad apple?" She said, "Yep," with no shame.

I couldn't entirely blame her resentment because I remembered a time coming out of an upscale breakfast restaurant. I had an untouched waffle leftover in a to-go container. I went driving to where I knew there were hungry and homeless people. The woman I was with at the time gave the box of warm, fresh food to a homeless guy as he was digging in a trash can. The homeless guy barked at us, saying, "Hey, what is it!?" with a rude and ungrateful tone. I thought, it doesn't matter what it is, just know there are not ants or bugs crawling through it. So I could sort of understand Sharmaine's grievance with the homeless community because some rude homeless person had made it difficult for others to want to give charity from their heart. Later that evening, I sent Sharmaine an image of a homeless man holding up a sign that read, "I'm sorry." We laughed about it, but I am an advocate of always giving to those in need when you have it to spare.

Sharmaine and I were a couple of weeks into our connection without any physical advancements yet. I found myself in a peculiar position because my family was taking a trip to Hawaii, and at the time of the booking I did not want to go without a female friend. I ended up inviting Nicole, who I had an on-and-off-again relationship with, to accompany me. Sharmaine happened to have a planned business trip to Hawaii at the same time I was going to be out there, but I was not traveling solo. The first couple of nights in Hawaii I hung out with my family and Nicole but the weekend came up, and Sharmaine was texting me, wanting to go out dancing. I hated to completely avoid her the whole time in Hawaii but Nicole was not going to let me out of sight. I felt bad that Sharmaine and I did not get to hook up at all, and I knew she must have found it strange that I could not break away from my family for one evening.

Sharmaine and I both made it back to San Diego at different times, and we met up at the mall to dine and see a movie. A month had passed by since we last saw each other, but the mutual interest was still in the air. As we walked through the parking garage to her car, we were talking on the side of the car, and the way she was looking at me urged me to kiss her. As soon as I kissed her, she said, "Finally. I was just about to tell you that I didn't know if we should continue because it seems like you aren't into me romantically." I told her I was interested in her; I just did not want it to move too fast. However, deep down inside I was so scared of screwing things up with Sharmaine that all of my steps were calculated down to every joke I told. I did not only like Sharmaine, but I also respected her as a young black woman chasing her dreams and making things happen for herself. Sharmaine was not the girl next door, or the average woman; she was wife material. A woman with class, humility, drive, and humor. I have never met a single woman with all of the qualities and talents that she had.

Once again, I was intimidated, but our connection made me love the challenge to step up and be a better man, or at least a complimentary addition to her life. I did a lot of forward thinking when it came to Sharmaine, but in the present neither of us were exclusive, and that topic was not on the table anytime soon for discussion. Sharmaine and I hung out a few more times until one weekend she went to Vegas with her girlfriends, and she realized something. What she realized was that she and I were better off just being friends. She sent me a text to officially demote me to her friendship zone. In her opinion, I was not physically engaging with her, and I didn't make a strong enough attempt to see her while we were both in Hawaii.

All the signs she was getting from me were telling her that I was not that into her romantically, but I was moving slow and over-calculating my steps to the point of cutting myself out of the game. I had turned basic arithmetic into college algebra. I forgot the fundamentals of winning a girl's heart. I pleaded with Sharmaine over the phone and through text messages to go on one final outing with me on my terms. And if we did not discover a mutual interest, I would gladly be the president of her friend-zone club. She was still hesitant, but she agreed to give me some scrap time on a Friday evening. She already had dinner plans with a friend, and we were going to be in the same area, so she agreed to meet up with me afterward. Women do this trick when they are not that interested in a guy anymore. Sharmaine set the night up so that whenever she decided to see me after her dinner plans, she could blame exhaustion for cutting my time down. I was completely aware of the trick, so I knew I had to get things moving fast to counter her plan.

I had Sharmaine meet me at a neighborhood bar; it was already 9:30 p.m. before she was freed up. I had already emptied a glass of wine, and had a glass awaiting her as she arrived. She walked in and had a simple, black dinner dress on, but anything she wore looked elegant on her. We chatted for a bit, and I charmed her to my best ability, then grabbed her hand and rushed her off to a lounge where music was playing and people were dancing. In a previous conversation with Sharmaine, she had told me that one thing she adores is when a man holds her hand and leads her through a large crowd. She probably thought that I was not listening when she had shared this. (Women do this all the time: drop little clues about simple things that rub them the right—or wrong—way.) The burden is on the guy to listen and respond accordingly, so at a later time he can collect "brownie points." I was subliminally collecting brownie points by being the aggressor and protector on that night. Sharmaine and I snagged a table and shared a bottle of wine. I liked her, and I could tell that she desired me back, but I had not been sexually assertive, and that was irritating her, to say the least. I was also aware that

Sharmaine was going away for a month or so for work around that time. I figured I would just give it my best shot to make some magic happen, so when she returned from her work trip, we could resume what we had started. Sharmaine was the perfect person to people watch and laugh with; we created a lot of fun, imaginary scenarios for people. It was natural for us just to laugh and relate to one another. Our outlook on life was similar, although we were yet to have a real in-depth conversation that dealt with the not-so-good parts of life like past hurts and disappointments. I knew we had the potential and the capability to build that depth.

As the disc jockey continued to play songs that were dance friendly, I pulled Sharmaine closer to me because I wanted to feel her hips sway to the beat of the music while we were face to face. I was feeling bold, and I felt like she was my girl that night. I said to her, "So you think we lack physical chemistry?"

"Well, you have not shown me considerable interest," she replied.

"I'm sorry. I over-calculated the situation."

"What does that mean?"

"I think that you are special, and girls of your caliber are a rare breed. I can honestly say that I have never met a woman like you. I think society overuses the phrase beauty and brains, and for me to adopt this phrase would be an understatement to describe you."

"Ha—look at you being Mr. Smooth tonight!"

"Hey, you are intimidating, but I'm here looking at you square in your face to tell you. I'm not scared. I just needed to regroup. And maybe a little push to feel confident that we're on the same page."

"Oh, is that right?

"Yes, and you owe me an apology as well."

"Whoa, for what?"

"You said we lack physical chemistry, and were not sure if you liked me in that way. Well, if that was true, why are you pressing your body against me, and why are you going to let me kiss you right here, right now?" I then started to kiss Sharmaine, and it was passionate, not drunk and sloppy. We then began to dance. Well, honestly, she had all the moves; I was just sticking to my two-step and admiring the chocolate goddess in my presence. We drank, laughed, danced, kissed, and repeated that cycle past midnight. We had a blast and headed back to her car. We were both tipsy, and she had a further drive home than I did, so she was concerned about it not being safe for her to drive. I gave her three choices: we hang out in the car until she sobered up; I could drive her home, and she could retrieve her vehicle in the morning; or I could drive us to my house, which is less than 5 miles away, and bring her back to her car in the morning. We decided to go back to my condo. I played R&B music on the way to my house as I was feeling sexual.

When we arrived at my place, she asked for a tee-shirt to sleep in, and jumped into my bed with just her tee-shirt and panties on. I followed the same dress code and turned out the lights. She was buzzing off the alcohol a bit and asked for a cup of water. Then she laid back and awaited my next move. I started to kiss her; her lips and tongue were soft and wet. I propped myself above her and placed my right hand between her thighs. She pulled her panties off her body. I immediately used my hand to check her sexual temperature, and she was soaking wet. She wanted me bad; she barely let me put my finger in her vagina before saying, "No, get a condom, and give me your penis." I reached for my drawer with the condoms, but my erection went away as my thoughts surfaced. I did not want alcohol to be the reason why we discovered our physical connection. I asked myself if she was going to regret sex in the morning. Did I just seduce her tonight because of my competitive spirit by her challenging our romantic chemistry? Once again, my mind had affected my performance. Why do I care about these women so much and their esteem? I kissed her on the cheek and said, "I don't know." She was silent. We both submerged under the covers without any undergarments on. I said goodnight. I was already regretting my decision, but I did not know how to recover. I was out of sync and could not catch my bearings.

We fell asleep, and I woke up to silence. Yes, it was awkward as I had left the night unresolved. I took her to her car, and she said she would text me later. Inevitably, Sharmaine sent me a 4-part text saying how embarrassing the night was, and how she wished to never hear from me again. She had never experienced that level of rejection. But her grounds for complaint were false. I knew I had dug myself into a deep hole and I did not want things to end on this note. I refuted her text and the notion that I rejected her. I had to at least disprove her impression of the night. Us not having sex has nothing to do with me wanting her, it is the opposite; once again, I wanted her too much. However, we were not in the right state of mind to have a sensible conversation, and I did not want alcohol to play a role in us taking this next step. I let Sharmaine know that I cherished everything about her, and I did not want to lose her as a friend. I stressed that cutting me off because of this misreading would be a mistake, but I would honor her sincere desire if she wanted no contact.

Fortunately, Sharmaine and I continued to text, but she was heading away for work for a few months. During her time away, we did not talk—maybe a few emails. When Sharmaine returned, I was off again with Nicole. I was happy and slightly surprised for Sharmaine to reach out to me to catch up. We scheduled a night to meet for dinner and a movie, but she wanted to select the film, and her choice was interesting. During dinner, we laughed and joked as always, which was good, because the last time I'd seen her getting out of my car, she was upset. She seemed to be vibrant and ready for a new chapter. We headed to the theater to see a film called *Addiction*. I was not familiar with this flick. The movie was an interesting selection because it turned out to be about a woman in a committed relationship who was addicted to sex to the point where it had disrupted her family and marriage. The movie had some heavy sex scenes that made my pants feel like they were on too tight.

Before the film began, Sharmaine unexpectedly, asked, "Do you mind if I facetime my boyfriend?" I was perplexed. It was strange timing, and the boyfriend was news. Before I could even reply, she was calling the guy, and she wanted me to meet him over the phone to reassure him that I was not a threat. I had not received the memo, but apparently, she had made me the friend-zone president after all. I was slightly perturbed, but particularly curious about why she'd invited me to such an erotic movie. To make matters worse, after the film, I was ready for crazy sex, but she made out like a bandit while the movie credits were rolling. Looking back, I think she was either trying to get even with me, or trying to regain an upper hand of some kind. She knew what she was doing— why did she not tell me about her boyfriend before meeting up? She made me feel like the gay friend escorting his sexy, female friend around. I ended up texting just to find out how the boyfriend thing had happened. Come to find out, this new guy had just made a strong attempt and got her. Most girls can be captured if the other person wants them bad enough and relentlessly pursues. You cannot let distance, social class, or any intimidating factors delay the execution of getting the person you desire. People like to be pursued with purpose, when it's fun, exciting, witty, and non-creepy.

Sharmaine's boyfriend, Cliff, lived seven driving hours away, so on the weekends she would see him, and my friendship time was diminishing. After the holidays, I called to tell her happy New Year and to find out if I could get some more friend time with her this year. When I called, she was actually at the airport heading to an exotic vacation with her boyfriend. I could not have called at a worse time. The good news came when she returned, and I found out there had been some turbulence while they were on their vacation. I never tried to be the guy whose goal is to break-up a relationship for my benefit. I believe in letting all relationships run their course, and letting things happen naturally. I had a friend performing at the House of Blues, and I invited Sharmaine. She showed up with a guy; I thought it was Cliff, but it was another male friend who was in town—she wanted to give him some time as well. He was cool, and we all had a great time.

Sharmaine and I got a chance to talk, and we took a selfie that turned out to be a perfect photo. I sent her the selfie later that night in a text after the event was over, and I said, "You cannot deny that we look good together." She agreed, and we had heard this before from many strangers while we were out in social settings. Sharmaine's relationship was getting rockier with Cliff, and she asked me to accompany her to a photo shoot she was modeling for. I thought this was kind of cool, even though I'm not into modeling as a career. We ended up spending the whole day together.

We did the photo shoot for 3-4 hours with only two wardrobe changes that had the theme "from the athlete to the woman". She took some shots in athletic wear and some pictures in a dress and heels on the football field. Sharmaine looked amazing, but I could see a little vulnerability. I was a good friend that day, supporting and giving honest feedback of the photos. During the photo shoot, I could not help but think I would be happy and ahead of most guys if I had just half the woman that Sharmaine was. We then headed to an outdoor farmer's market in Oceanside, CA. We ate great food and walked around sharing food and each other's space. She wanted to stop at her friend's house and deliver a dessert and wine bottle to her that we had picked up. We visited at her friend's house for two hours, and the discussion came up concerning why I hadn't closed the deal with Sharmaine. The friend wanted to know how I felt now looking in from the outside? Her friend was respectful, but brutally honest. It left me feeling pretty defeated that night. On the car ride back home, I confessed to Sharmaine that I had messed up by not following through in a few ways. She did not have a response.

A couple of weeks later, Sharmaine called me after an argument with her boyfriend. While he was in the background, she told me that he does not cherish her. I thought this was weird and a definite no-no. You cannot complain to another man about your boyfriend while you are in the relationship while he is in your presence. I could tell that both of them were a bit tipsy, and maybe just in a mode to push each other's buttons, but she still had the longing to reach out to me in distress. It was hard for me to believe that Cliff and Sharmaine got along better than us. We were like peanut butter and jelly. Our philosophies and humor were similar, and made it easy to want to be around each other. Our conversation was consistently superb like Steph Curry's 3-point shot. We just never had pillow talk, and Cliff had the sexual upper hand on me because I was yet to partake in Sharmaine's chocolate ocean.

One night after my rehearsal, I got the call that I had been waiting for from Sharmaine. She called me sad and cried over the passing of her Grandmother—no, I was not happy to hear that kind of news. I was glad that I was part of her support group, and she was leaning on me to comfort her, and just be a rock in this tough time for her. If a person does not trust you with their tears and pain, then you cannot claim that you are close to that person. I said what I had to say to give her support and keep her emotionally stable. She called me the day after visiting with family and just wanted to hang out with me to take her mind off of things. I did not know what happened to Cliff and did not care; I was the man of the moment. We met downtown for dinner. She was wearing a sexy, revealing top and tight pants. At the restaurant, some

Navy recruits were celebrating a graduation of some sort, and it was entertaining alone just laughing at their drunken antics. We had fun reacting to the foolish things their table was doing. They had to have toasted their glasses at least a hundred times to every little thing, and everyone had slurred speech during their toast.

The night was relaxed, and there was no expectation or even big conversation. I ordered dessert, drank a glass of wine, and watched Russell Westbrook highlights on the TV screen above. Then someone saw us through the window of the restaurant and brought in a flyer advertising a new hookah lounge around the corner. We gazed at the flyer, then both said that we had never smoked Hookah. I had never smoked anything. Sharmaine suggested we go and check out the scene; I just wanted to hang out more. As we were walking to the lounge, she suggested that we be bold and daring. I said, "What do you have in mind?" She said, "Let's have a first-ever moment together." I said, "Okay, but I'm going to need to a few shots before embarking on this adventure." Sharmaine said, "You pay for shots, and I'll pay for the hookah experience." We got lucky because we found this lovely sofa and table in the corner with dim lighting. We immediately claimed that spot for the night. I was feeling loose and daring. We also wanted to be incognito because we needed a tutorial from the staff on how it works, and it is embarrassing not knowing exactly what you are doing. However, we got the hang of it fast.

We got a tropical flavor, and started taking turns and performing tricks with the smoke. I felt a nice buzz, and the music was playing; everything was just flowing ideally. We began to mingle with another guest, and I even saw a few friends that I knew, but I wanted my space to be one-on-one with Sharmaine. I inhaled a long breath of smoke, and Sharmaine wanted me to exhale in her mouth— "a kiss hit." She then jumped on top of me while I was sitting back on the sofa and started kissing me. We immediately mentally left the room and went to a magical, sexual place. We were tongue kissing, and I was feeling on her, and I could tell she wanted me while her body was all over mine. We finally took a breath, and she pulled out her phone and started filming us just being silly and sexual. She began to dance for me while I was on the sofa. People were mesmerized by her presence and seductive moves. I almost felt like I was dreaming because everything was flawlessly flowing. I sincerely loved laughing with her just as much as kissing her. We decided to leave, and she insisted on giving me a ride to my car. She had parked in a parking garage, and as we made it to her car door, I grabbed her. "Hey, it was getting heated in the lounge. Was that just the hookah talking? Are you done expressing how you were feeling? I'm not."

She said, "No, I like the way you made me feel tonight. You showed me a side of you I that I haven't seen before."

"Well, there is still more for you to see and touch." I took her hand and placed it on the front inside of my pants. I wanted her to know that I wanted all of her right then and there. She gasped while firmly groping my stuff, followed by a kiss and biting my bottom lip. I opened up her car door, and I said, "I dare you to be bad tonight with me, gorgeous." Sharmaine grabbed my shirt and pulled me into the car with her. We started to go at it, kissing intensely, and removing our clothes. The car windows were steaming, and I felt charged and untouchable. I opened her sunroof, and propped her up above the shoulders of the front car seats. I turned her back to the dashboard while her head was out of the sunroof. I sat in the middle back seat, face to face with her chocolate flavored vagina. I kissed her inner thigh as she anticipated every touch.

My hands were holding up her bottom, and as I began to lick her in the middle, her legs shot out into a v shape. She had placed one hand on the back of my head to guide me to the spots where she wanted me to stick my tongue deeper inside. I could tell I was satisfying Sharmaine by the way her chocolate lava cake was pouring out of her, warm and wet. She started to get louder, and being in the parking garage, the noise became arousing...but also easily detectable. I had to pull her down back into the car. I sat her in the best seat in the car, right on top of my full erection. She slid right down my pole as my hands were guiding her ass. Sharmaine settled into a nice rhythm that was medium tempo. I could hear the sound of my penis and her moist vagina engaging. I asked her if she had been waiting for this kind of attention from me. She replied, "Oh yeah, but now I'm going to make you pay for delaying the delivery."

As soon as she said that, her tempo increased to a level that I had to just hold on for the ride. She was working me from every angle. The sweat had built up as if we were in a sauna. She then told me to shut up and take this royal pussy. Her confidence blew me away. I do not mind when people are cocky and they can back it up. As the intercourse was progressing, I wanted a chance to lead, so I tapped her to get up and lie down on the back seats. I threw one of her legs over my shoulder as I re-entered inside of her from the top view.

I just wanted to hump her and work her as if we had hit the hydraulics switch in the car. There was passion behind each thrust; I thought she was the most amazing woman I have ever come across. It's funny because society always talks about women trapping wealthy men into impregnating them so they can either get married or gain financial support for 18 years. Sharmaine was the type of woman who a man would want to fertilize so they could have a chance to be connected to her for life. Sorry, but guys think the same way; it's just not financially motivated. Men like having someone sexy and smart.

As our sex session continued, she insisted that I fuck her with one leg elevated until she climaxed. As she orgasmed, she wanted me to stroke her harder, then she said make me cum twice. I turned her sweet chocolate ass around and went deeper. Not too wild—I wanted to give her deep, close, and controlled strokes. I found a medium smooth rhythm, and I started to talk nasty to her. I said, "Sharmaine, relax your body because we are about to peak together." I wanted us to get into the same breathing pattern and similar motion. Our bodies got into harmony, and we became more in tune. Sharmaine went from the sound of just breathing to a loud orgasmic moan, and as she started to cum the second time I could feel my impending ejaculation. Sweat dripped down my chin and my legs trembled with anticipation. Sharmaine says, "Release all of your cream in me, baby," and I said, "I'm about to bust." As I started to ejaculate, Sharmaine pulled me a couple of inches out of her pussy where the head of my penis was barely inside of her. She began to slowly feed my penis inside of her while massaging my testicles as my seeds released. I could not help myself—the pleasure boost forced me to let out a roar. She even took my reserve tank. I could not muster the energy to even stand. After we collected ourselves, we were both drained and giggly.

Sharmaine turned to me, and in a mildly regretful tone, said, "What did you just do to me? I have a boyfriend."

"Boyfriend!?"

"Well, we are on-and-off."

"I hope tonight you guys are *off* because tonight you were *on* with me. Literally on me, doing some naughty things."

"Damn, Anthony, you confuse me so much. Sorry, but I have to go."

Sharmaine did not choose to continue experimenting with the idea of us being an item. I guess she was in too deep with her on-again-off-again relationship. Maybe Sharmaine thought that who I initially showed her was the guy who I planned to be. I was reserved, slow to action, and not captivating her sexual attention. I also thought Sharmaine was a brilliant woman, and she had to be the type of person who contemplates the future and chooses the right stock to invest in. Unfortunately, love and infatuation can make the smartest people do the stupidest things. Some women are attracted to guys who need them, or people they can transform into what they think is a better version. There are smart women in this modern day who are in abusive relationships that they cannot untangle from. What is the connection that keeps people glued together even when it is unhealthy? Is it that we think the good ol' days from the beginning of the relationship are going to return again? When it comes to dating and relationships, we are too foolish to see the truth, even when it's bad six days a week. We hang on and defend the one seventh good day.

I never asked Sharmaine to choose me or drop everyone and give me her undivided attention. I sold myself short. I met a beautiful woman, who was more accomplished than me at the time, and I let it defeat me instead of making her mine and growing with her until my day came when I could stand beside her. I hate that it impacted my psyche and self-value. I know better; the woman I wanted would never stand a man without confidence, drive, and vigor. Sharmaine might have been my biggest choke job. I had her attention and friendship, and our head connection finally converted into a bed connection. In spite of the investment and mental compatibility, I never uttered the critical words that make people stay in tough times. I never said, "Sharmaine, I want you."

Everybody wants to feel wanted or at least hear they are wanted. With Sharmaine, I planted the seed on fertile soil in the sun, but forgot to water the seed. It is often the simple things we forget to say or do that can make a person frown or stray.

CONCLUSION

A person cannot find love unless they make their mind and heart available. There are many obstacles to overcome to capitalize on the awesome journey of real romance and physical intimacy, but the biggest obstacle is self. My first piece of advice is to stay within your limitations and stimulate the mind. Everyone is not complicated, and everyone is not simple. I also found out through my own sexual journey that I am more complicated than what I preferred, and maybe even more complicated than what some of my former or potential sex partners would have preferred. I live in my head too much, and the best fit for me is someone who is highly intelligent and who is capable of stimulating my mind as well. I care about how I am perceived by my relationship partner. Even though I have some cut-throat attributes, I have issues framing sex as just sex in my mind. I have always desired to get everything else, then the pussy, like D.J Quik said. Nevertheless, captivating the mind has always been the key to advancing romance with the female sex. Some guys care about being understood more than being physically enticed as well. Sticks and stones do break bones and words do hurt. However, words can shift the momentum and crack the code. When a person says, I can no longer be with you because you broke my heart; they are saying you are not who you said you are or who they thought you were. When your opinion of your lover or friend changes, you do not only have a mind change, but you hold them in a new regard that is less favorable.

Men can be too focused on arousing the body instead of the mind. I do not want my readers to think that stimulating the mind has to be a complicated task. It is like everything else when advertising or soliciting, you have to know your audience. As a young man, I would tune into the Howard Stern radio show or similar stations where the host flirts with a sexy female guest and would rarely get rejected by the gorgeous women. Howard did not have to say anything intellectual to get his guest to flirt back. Sometimes just being humorous is enough to make the other person respond or just saying something daring can gain the interest of others. Maybe I should have mentioned earlier in the book that some women still have a childlike mentality, where they are just happy to be with the cool guy, even if their man's conversation is not smarter than a fifth grader.

I knew a guy who always had a beautiful looking girl on his shoulder, and his strategy was just to diminish the qualities of the woman he was pursuing or dating. If she were stunning with an exotic look, he would say, "You have this different look about you that makes you cute." Even though the girl was a "ten," he would treat her like she was a "seven." Some women's self-esteem depends on the person they are dating. Is the person they are in a relationship with treating them like expensive china or plastic Tupperware? However, many women are changing the game, and they recognize their value and potential on their own. My same friend would make the ladies he is with think they were substandard to him on a psychological level which made them slow to speak. Let's be honest, this type of strategy is someone who wants to control and needs their partner to feel inferior to them to compensate for their own shortcomings. Arousing the mind is not about brainwashing, but there is a way to get a strong and healthy edge.

A healthy conversation comes natural and sometimes you have to accept losses like gains. I was on a panel for an audition once, and there was a woman named Krystle who completed a decent audition, but I was struck by how beautiful she was, and how much class came across during the audition. As she finished up, I escorted her out the door and could not hold my tongue. I said, "I cannot take the chance of our paths not crossing again. Yes, you did an excellent job in the audition, and you may be called back. However, I would sincerely regret it if I did not at least ask you for your phone number so I can contact you for my personal interest." Krystle gave me her number, and I told her I would call her later that day if she were free. I did because I do not believe in playing the 48-hours waiting game. I called her later that evening, and we talked. Well, she talked; I listened. Krystle discussed politics, religion, black history, and more. Krystle had a lot of information to share, but I felt her goal was to either run me away with her passion for such topics, or she was testing me to see what I had to offer to her preferred conversational topics. Needless to say, I was not prepared or enthused about having this in-depth conversation on the first night. Yes, Krystle was educated and beautiful, and even though I can hold my own with very smart people, I accepted my loss and did not contact Krystle again, nor do I think Krystle wanted me to call her again. Krystle could have been looking for someone who was on the cerebral level with her, but I was not the one, at least at that time. Krystle may have been projecting an assumed incompatibility with her, and she staged the phone conversation to prove to herself, or me, that I was not in her league. I do not believe Krystle would have had the same conversation if she thought I was a professional person or if she did not see me in an inferior light. Perhaps I am wrong, and maybe she is a big conversationalist with touchy topics. Needless to say, Krystle and I were not a natural match.

Where people often go wrong is they know they are not a good fit for a person at the time of meeting them, but because of ego, greed, or a pattern of dishonesty, people refuse to bow out respectfully and continue to fake the funk. I have accepted that all women do not find me attractive or like my personality. However, I believe a person can always be in play by sneaking through the physiological backdoor. When you subtly surprise a person with your intelligence, you hear them say, "Oh, I did not know that you knew that, or "I would have never thought you had this much information about this topic." Many types of dating can take on the form of speed dating with rapid disclosure on passionate topics of interest. However, speed dating is not just laying your resume on the table in 90 seconds, or a time to sit back and image if you would have cute kids with the person you just met on the other side of the table. Speed dating is successful when you like the discussion, and it's moving at a pace that is comfortable and satisfying for all parties. Yes, women want their partners to be active listeners, and men want women to make sense, from our perspective. However, all want to be understood and to have someone who brings value to the conversation.

One of the negotiating tactics that law enforcement uses is communicating on a physiological level that the criminal can comprehend and make a connection. It is not (generally) a good outcome if the negotiator is talking above or below, but speaking right at a level that the person can feel what they are saying is of value, and it is accurately received. There are conversational needs that we all desire for our partner to meet. With all of the women I date, I make sure that good conversation will be a strength. In a conversation between possible love interests, the number one thing is a connection. The pairing needs to be a connection through a similar interest in sports, art, music, science, education, career, movie taste, sensitivity, or humor. People like others who think like them—this is how many become friends. Some people are friends just because they root for the same sports team. The friends that you truly value are not just the ones who brought the avocado dip to the Super Bowl party. Friends gain value when they give you good career tips or relationship advice. We rely on our core friends to keep us grounded, and to provide sound advice when we cannot think straight, or our judgment is nebulous.

At the time, with Ashley, I felt we had gained a unique bond because she was able to be vulnerable with me, and display the things that she previously thought she should shun because I might run away. If true, it was not too much that I was her first sexual encounter, but the fact that she was able to be herself and be accepted, which included inexperience, curiosity, awkwardness, courage, passion, and fear of caring for someone in a meaningful way.

Identification is an important factor in making a connection. People recognize, identify, and are more comfortable with certain types of personalities, or cultures. Even if someone is not the same culture or race does not prevent connection. Like I mentioned earlier in the chapter, as an African American man, I understand and accept that not all women will be attracted to me just because of my skin tone. We all have our stereotypes that make us hesitant or think twice before action. But despite our apprehensions, an intellectual connection can overcome the stereotypes. Diversity is good for the kitchen, just like it is great in the bedroom. An open mind creates opportunities for new thrills and new joys. To evolve as a society, we have to step out of our comfort zone and embrace things that are different and harmless. I recently had to buy doughnuts for my cost/price contract analysis class I had to take for work. There were 30 classmates, and I knew that glazed was the standard doughnuts choice. What people tend to rely on is familiarity because it is the safe selection and low-risk choice. However, I like things that offer variety.

Different cultures have different definitions of romance. Different age groups have a different definition of love and affection. Of course, different sexes have their own interpretation of love. We say music is a universal language, but so is love and arousal. Arousing through the many senses, including the often-overlooked ear canal is an emphasis I want to leave with you. The ear canal is a powerful conduit to the imagination. Most times when I imagine something, it is because of something I heard not saw. As an American man, I am not aroused by French accents and some other foreign accents. Why? Because I find it unappealing when a woman melts just because she heard a French accent. Society has programmed us to think and feel that romance is a French or Spanish culture invention. There are many, but a fairly recent example was in the movie *Along Came Polly* when Debra Messing's character leaves Ben Stiller's character while on their honeymoon for a guy with an accent. Possibly the way the words blend into each other and do not jump—like the game of hopscotch in the English language—is what makes women so crazy over the tone, phrasing, and dialect. Through my experiences, though, I have failed to understand the power of the tongue and the impact of what a woman hears. To be fair, men have their weak-in-the-knees accents as well, especially African-American men. When having sex with a Puerto Rican or Latino female, if she says anything in her native language or something along the lines of, "Give it to me, Papi" it's likely to make a man go ballistic—in the good way. So, yes, men are easily aroused by accents as well. Remember Hanna had an Australian accent that made her overall rating jump through the roof because of that factor. An accent alone can make a person unique and pursued in the American culture. I have always had a theory that fancy restaurants prefer to hire people with accents because of the perception of accents associated with upper class and royalty. I have been to many upscale restaurants where the waiter is faking an accent so he can play the part. However, everyone does not have the accent to arouse our potential mates, but we do have words that can shape a relationship or set up sexual encounters.

In relationships caring is the sharing of words, not just being flashy with material items or having a charming accent. Mature women don't tend to care about the car model you're driving them around in on the first date; they are more concerned about having an adult conversation that they can enjoy. I realized that a mature woman would be happier riding in my six-year-old coupe with a nice, flowing conversation than a luxury SUV with a driver who only wants to discuss the next *Avengers* movie. Yes, actions do speak louder than words, but not for everyone. Some people need to hear it before they see it. Hearing kind words or words to spark the heart can get the engine started between the legs. And lying in bed with someone who understands you makes you want to go for round two or three. We *settle* for people who have a heartbeat and the desired body parts to help us reach our climax, but it's easier to reach the maximum heights of arousal with someone who stimulates us intellectually. Without that, it's little more than what I tend to call one-and-done because, after that orgasm, you don't want to cuddle or hear the other person snore throughout the night. Why do people creep out right after, or in the middle of the night? There is no connection. People do not want to be forced to talk if it isn't a natural conversation. Nowadays, when I see couples who, from the outside, do not appear to be equally matched based on physique or attractiveness I know it was likely their intellectual compatibility that paired them up.

What I have learned is that sex can happen because of a fluke, a good day, or desperate situation, but repeated sex with your desired partner can only occur when the cerebral comes before the physical. Looking back, I discovered that in my younger years I was missing the importance of the intellectual connection. Some people need their partner to be in tune with them on a mental level, not so much emotional. Not everyone is in sync with their emotions, and they tend to lead by the mind instead of the heart or gut. Men are often defined as pursuers who only care if the person has two legs and a hole to put their junk inside. However, many men look for security and psychological security as well. If a man is unappreciated or feels their partner is not socially inclined, he is only going to engage for so long, and not consider the person for a long-term commitment. We do not necessarily need to be heard and understood as much as a female companion, but we need to know that what we have is a good stock to invest in before moving forward. Intellect may not be the key component to getting a guy in bed, but may be key in getting us to the altar. Everyone's goal is not marriage, or even sex, but both feel so much better when the mind is connected.

Bonus Chapter

You, Me, and Him?

I have always had a general rule that many people understand and honor, which is not to date neighbors or coworkers. This rule can be difficult for men to follow, but it saves a ton of head and heartache. In high school, it was normal to be stuck in a class with an attractive person for six hours a day, and it was ok to date that person—walk from class to class holding hands with everyone on campus knowing who you're going steady with, at least for that semester. However, those rule change as you become an adult. Dating a coworker or neighbor is forbidden in my book. Why? The obvious can go wrong, and most likely will go wrong. It is best only to befriend your neighbor or coworker even if they are irresistible. Use the friendship to date your friend's attractive friends. You do not want to fall in love with a neighbor or coworker because when the relationship comes to a conclusion, it is going to feel like salt getting poured into your love wound every time you see that neighbor or coworker go out with another person; furthermore, bring home another person.

Dating a coworker can also become unprofessional in the workplace. It is a high possibility that disagreements will spill over into the office environment. I have always enjoyed working away from my love interest because space to miss one another is great for a relationship. Dating someone in the same company, however, is different from dating someone in the same office. As a whole, the company is larger with various departments and facilities for a person to have independent interaction with others. Yes, rules are made to be broken, but people don't tend to learn from the rules they break, and it backfires. I do have the discipline to befriend attractive coworkers and not cross the line with them. I do not consider myself a greedy man or feel subjected to chasing every cute individual that crosses my path. Working in a small office with four women as a single young man, I maintained professional and courteous behavior. Yes, it is easy to get drawn into a coworker's personality after spending nine hour days with them for months or years. Happy-hour is popular among colleagues, people sometimes flirt and test the line. No, not me.

I recall a time, at the office setting I just mentioned, when the office manager hired another woman to join our already small staff and I thought that it might be challenging because throwing new energy into our copacetic mix might rock the boat. Well, Lacey was the new girl from New York with a little bit of flavor to her because of that natural east coast vibe. Lacey was also married to a physician assistant; she had two kids, a dog, a wonderful house, but was re-entering the workforce after a 10-year hiatus taking care of the family. I was pretty much friendly with all the women in the office, but I have always tried to have more than just surface conversations. If I am going to work with someone closely, I want to know their temperament and personality type so I know how to blend with and address them accordingly. Lacey and my friendship built up as the weeks grew to months. One day our supervisor signed us both up to go to a training seminar in downtown San Diego for a topic that was related to our job. The training was a two-day course, but we didn't mind having to go because our job had mandated training hours that we must achieve annually.

Lacey and I sat next to each other in the class, as we did not know anyone else in the class session. As the day progressed, the subject became less appealing, so we started to text each other, even though we were sitting one seat from another. The content of our text messages went quickly from how boring this class was to I like what you're wearing today. Lacey did have the type of blue eyes that can put a mini-spell on a person if they stare into them for too long. Lacey was Caucasian with Irish and Italian mixed in her bloodline. She was only five-foot-tall with no shoes, but had an excellent shape, and maybe some enhancement in the chest region. Ultimately, her body was evenly proportioned, and she had a ton of confidence. Lacey referred to herself as a "fun-size." I did not know what that meant, but she immediately explained it to me, saying her body type is small enough to pick-up and maneuver, or toss around for her partner's pleasure. As the flirting launched, it was more interesting than the training course, but what made it more thriving is that we were next to each other and able to see one another's physical reactions after reading the text.

Lacey and I were connecting as two mature and intelligent adults. It did not take me long to ask why she was flirting with me when she has such a perfect life at home. Are you just playing around to help the time pass by easier or are you not getting this kind of attention at home? Lacey was quick to say, "Hey, I can look and talk, as long as I don't touch then we are still in the clear." As we came upon our lunch break, we decided to take a walk down the street to a park bench. As we sat on the bench and it was time to face each other while speaking aloud, there was some blushing on her end. I asked her what was up. She said I do just want a little hug from you. I said, "Okay, we can do that," but as soon as we embraced I knew there might be trouble. For me, it was cool flirting to help the time pass, but Lacey was a married woman who, in my eyes, should not even have an interest in me. I knew from looking at her family photos on her work desk that I could not provide the lifestyle that her husband had established. The lunch break ended and we hugged again, both knowing that something more could easily happen, but neither of us was foolish enough to go that far.

The next day, the office staff had plans to have a happy hour meet up after the training downtown. When Lacey reported to the training, she immediately said that she could not stop thinking about the hug and how much I made her smile. I told Lacey that I try my best to always be honest with my feelings, especially when I have nothing to lose. I said,

"Lacey, your marriage is probably stagnant, and you just need a little jump start to get it moving back in the right direction. Fooling with me will only cause trouble and confusion." She thought about it for a moment, then said, "My husband and I have thought about opening up our marriage anyways." When Lacey said that to me, it did catch my attention for a minute, then my judgment kicked in. I did not want to be the test pilot on someone's marriage boundaries or experiments. Lacey and I went to lunch again on the same park bench. This time she reached for my hand while I was sitting there. I think whenever you are sneaking around, in that moment, things are enhanced and seem better or even right, yet it is human nature to get a rush of adrenaline in high-risk situations.

After the training, we had to change our behavior and demeanor. We did not want our coworkers to detect any misbehaving. We were eager, like two teenage sweethearts, and I was hoping that by adding alcohol we would not get careless. It was not long before our coworker Lauryn spotted us playing footsie under the table like too horny birds. Lauryn just brought it out to everyone's attention, and said, "Why are you too playing footsie under the table? Did we miss something?" Lacey froze up, like I knew she would, because just a couple weeks ago she was the "innocent" soccer mom, so I said, "I was trying to get her attention about this inside joke. However, the joke was rude, so my bad."

Later that evening, Lacey sent me a thank you text for covering her. She did not want anyone to know about our flirting. Lacey also would never want to embarrass her family, but Lacey was in a position that many married women find themselves in as a result of getting married too young. Lacey had been married to Thompson since she was 21, and had never really had the chance to live the single life exploring and having fun. By age 25, Lacey had two kids and was following Thompson around to benefit his career. In the meantime, she was an attentive mother who earned a graduate degree and kept in shape. However, Lacey was still curious and never got to exhaust her young, fun, and daring side. On the surface, Lacey and I were careful never to seem like we were that into each other, but because we were so different racially and socially, we came together with the intent to learn about the other person, and fulfill the parts that either of us lacked. We did not stop flirting when we returned to work. We started to email each other, and every time she got up to go to the restroom she would give me this look of seduction in passing. Once again, the secrecy from the coworkers made what Lacey and I had more stimulating in our eyes. Lacey did have a deep thought process and would love to email me "what if" scenarios. Playing make believe with me was a happy place for her.

After having met Thompson a few times, it was difficult for me to grasp the reasoning behind Lacey being unfulfilled. There is a difference when in a relationship that a person is unfulfilled vs. unhappy. Being unfulfilled in a relationship can be that your partner is missing an element that makes things complete. The element could be that since you have been with this partner their job has taken priority over the relationship. Or your partner has not been attentive towards the relationship because he or she is caring for their elderly or ill parent. This oversight is repairable, and through communication and proper planning, things can turn around for the couple. On the other side of the equation, a person can feel unfulfilled if they think their talents and strengths are being unused or unappreciated in the relationship. This sort of feeling of un-fulfillment can be healed by your partner taking a personal interest in you as a distinct individual, or likewise, taking in interest in your partner in those ways and showing appreciation. When a person is unhappy in a marriage or relationship, they are not just undervalued from their perspective but also unappreciated and possibly mistreated. When a person cannot see things getting better, the unhappiness turns into emotional abandonment which is difficult to recover from without pursuing a change in purpose. Self-awareness in a relationship is looking at what contributions you are making that are purely beneficial for your partner only. Sometimes it needs to be about your partner and them only. Also, knowing the thing that you are doing that can be damaging to the relationship. Lacey was not unhappy in her marriage, just unfulfilled. She was always in wife or mommy mode, and sometimes she wanted to be the girlfriend—the lady with fewer responsibilities, being pursued by her man. I did come to find out that Thompson had a very relaxed personality, so if Lacey said she was going out with the girls and would not be home until the wee hours in the morning, Thompson would not be bothered, concerned, or object. Even though Lacey preferred a secure man, that security or relaxed style can also come across as disinterest. After 12 years of marriage with Thompson, she felt like she had kept her end of the bargain; she had remained attractive, savvy, and hustled for her household. However, Thompson did too, and he was available for the kids needs and was a great provider to maintain a comfortable life for his family. Lacey was still unfulfilled, though, because of the unspoken love problems. These problems are quiet storms that hide, and sometimes fester, in a relationship.

For example, a person says they feel like they lost the core of who they were or wanted to be since staying in the relationship. There are many women, mostly mothers, who sacrifice their dreams and goals for the benefit of the family. In those sacrifices, sometimes you lose the fabric of who you are. Lacey wanted Thompson to make her feel a certain way overall. This is common and important in all relationships. Your partner can influence your self-esteem in a negative way if there are no words of affirmation or validation. Even if you have a stay-at-home spouse, there needs to be encouraging words and acknowledgement of the contribution the person is bringing to the household and relationship.

The other twist to my surprise about Lacey being into me was that you can be attracted to someone while in a committed relationship. Lacey failed to cut communications once she recognized that there could be potential sparks. Yes, it is wrong to engage on both sides, but it appeared to me that I had the green light from her *and* Thompson. I ran into both of them one night in a late-night neighborhood lounge. I chatted with them, and other party members, and then Lacey followed me to the restroom. She started kissing me—yes, we were both a little influenced by alcohol, but I was not comfortable with our first kiss being on a night where her husband and friends were in the same building. I was starting to understand that she was the type of lady who lives for a moment's thrill. I quickly rushed back to the group. I noticed back at the table that the hostess was giving Thompson extra attention. Thompson enjoyed the flirtatiousness from the hostess. He was not a bad looking guy, and he had other qualities that I am sure most women would cherish.

 As the night progressed, I started to blend in well in the conversation with Lacey, Thompson, and their friends. They even invited me over for a night-cap, and I went over to hang out at their house. We laughed and drank wine, and Lacey discreetly flirted, making suggestive gestures to me all night long. As I was leaving, Thompson said to me that he would love to go out just the two of us to flirt with the ladies in town. He said, "I would make a great wingman." The funny thing was I could see him and I enjoying each other's company and forming a great one- two combo. A black and white male, both young and professional, winning the ladies over. The difficult thing I could not wrap my brain around was that his wife and I were on the verge of screwing each other. Lacey excused herself to walk me out to the car. I was hoping she was not going to make a move on me because her kids or friends could easily peek out of their window and catch us in the act. Lacey was happy to see how well I was able to integrate into her world, and it made her admire and desire me even more. One night, a week later, Lacey and I, by chance, were the last ones to lock up the office. She had been emailing me all afternoon because she knew that everyone's schedule had them leaving us behind for the day. Lacey was hoping to get a goodbye hug and kiss because at that point, at work, I was her man. Even though Thompson would often come by to take her to lunch, she always made me feel like she would have preferred to just sit around the table and eat with me. That day, as we were set to leave, I went to her desk to escort her out. "Are you ready to go?" I asked.

"Yes, do you have my hug?"

"Of course."

As I hugged her, she kissed me on the neck, and for some reason that is a sensitive spot for me that I do not share with anyone because I feel like that's a feminine spot, and I am all man!

"See, there you go starting stuff," I said.

"You know you don't want me to stop."

We started kissing, and I fondled her ass. She started to breathe harder while biting my bottom lip. She was rubbing my head, then reached for my penis. I had a maximum erection bulging out of my pants. I turned her around and lifted up her skirt as her ass pressed up against my dick. I started to kiss her on her neck from the backside. I slid my hands down into her panties to find that she was completely groomed.

"No, no, bad boy—you can't get it all right here."

"Damn, why are you getting me this excited to just let me down? Let's get out of here to prevent more damage."

I grabbed her hand, and she grabbed her things. We started to leave. Then she said, "Lock the door and turn off the lights. I want to feel it outside of your pants. Come on, I can take it, my husband has a girthy penis, and I can show you some of the things I can do with it."

"Lacey, I have a rule. I never bring my dick out unless I know it is going to get wet somehow."

After I locked and closed the door, Lacey pulled me over to our coworker's desk. She leaned me against the edge of the desk, pulled my pants down, and put my penis in her mouth. She was working me hard, and pulling me deeper down her throat. I was not only turned on by the sound of her tongue waxing my chocolate stick, but by the sight of her eyes looking like the Hawaiian ocean view. As I looked down on her while she was on her knees pleasing me, I found her expression of submission to have an enormous impact on my arousal and was wildly seductive. I knew she was a pro, and very modest about her skills. This former soccer mom had my testicles in her mouth, looking up and moaning while simultaneously jacking me off. As I moaned due to the exquisite pleasure, she gave it to me more. I said, "You're going to make me cum." Then Lacey put her mouth over my penis and swallowed all of the juice from me while groaning in a sensual way. My leg almost gave out on me, as she had exceeded my expectations.

Following that office performance, I was on a mission to get her in bed. After experiencing how well she gave oral sex, I needed her on top of me. The next week Lacey told me she and Thompson got into an argument over us. I asked why, and she said she told him about sucking my dick. I was upset and dumbfounded about why Lacey would tell her husband. She saw me getting angry, and quickly said, he doesn't care that I sucked your dick, he's upset that we were careless at our place of employment and put our careers at risk. "Well, I guess he has a point there," I said. I still did not trust that he would be ok with this. I remembered the Richard Gere and beautiful Diane Lane movie *Unfaithful.* I did not want to experience her husband's wrath because I'm sure his passion for their relationship outweighed mine. Thompson may be ok with her messing around with me today, but that does not mean that tomorrow he will not change his mind. Some people talk mess to their spouse and act like they would not care if the other fooled around on them. It is not until the individual's brain starts to draft unfavorable thoughts like, *I wonder if my wife kissed my kids after she sucked that other man's dick?* Even though Lacey told me it was OK and that we had the green light, I did not trust that things would work out fine, so I was hesitant to engage any further.

It was not until I ran into Thompson in the elevator at my job, and he initiated the hello and asked how I was doing that I started to feel better. I did not sense any animosity or jealousy. My position started to become relaxed once I saw for myself that Thompson was not disturbed. However, things were still a bit strange to me. Probably because I am not the type of man who would share my lady. I recall Lacey calling me one time close to midnight, furious because Thompson had not returned home after a happy hour with his friends. I asked her why she was so upset. "Even if he is out flirting with other ladies, why do you have this reaction knowing your own indiscretions?" She said, I just do not want him messing around with anyone tonight. Again, I asked, "Why?" She couldn't give me a logical or principled answer. Lacey was just selfish and jealous. I guess it did not feel too good for her being the one at home while your partner is out swindling. Lacey went out and checked every neighborhood hangout spot and finally located him. She stormed into the place where he was mingling and pulled him out. Then she sent me a text message later that night saying she was going to bed, and Thompson's drunk ass was lying next to her.

The following day I told her that she was sending me mixed signals, and that it really seemed like she just wanted her husband's attention and had deceitfully brought me in as a tool to get him to notice her. "The truth is," I said to her, "You are not ready to open up your marriage because the moment Thompson was willing to play ball you came in like a black tarp to cover the field as if there was a rain delay. You cannot handle Thompson putting his dick or tongue in another woman's pussy. But the worst thing about it is, you cannot bear your husband giving another woman more attention or consideration than he gives you. You are probably bothered when your husband does not notice when you change hairstyles or fragrances. Face it, Lacey, Thompson is your choice, whether you think he is a sorry ass or not. You two being in a happy or dysfunctional marriage is fine with me. You both said I do. It's just time for me to back off."

Lacey professed that she loved Thompson, but she had fallen in love with me. I did not respond to those claims. Shortly after my no reply, she sent me a naked picture of her. The photo was flawless. She was in a champagne colored room, lying on a gold couch as if she was floating down from a swing. The placement of the shot was perfect, and her breasts were perky with glitter sprinkled on her. The only thing she had on was a necklace. Like a weak man, I was sucked back into her plot. I said, "If you are serious about wanting us to be involved, I'm coming to pick you up, and we are going to do whatever I want tonight." Lacey agreed. I ended up meeting her out at a wine bar, and we talked and flirted until I got restless and I was ready for her to come back to my place. Lacey insisted on going to her place because her husband was gone and we were only a mile or two from her house. As we arrived at her house, I was a little fearful because I was not on home turf and we were up to risky business. I was not going to lay in the bed that her and her husband share, I do not care how tipsy or horny we both were.

As soon as we entered her house, she invited me into her guest bedroom. She took her clothes off, just leaving her panties and bra on. Lacey had on a thong, and she was ready for me to spank that ass. She then jumped into my arms, and wrapped her legs around my waist. I kissed her on her neck, and I had her in the air pressed up against the wall. She told me that she was ready and wanted me to fuck her on the wall. Lacey got down and pulled my pants down, then shoved my dick into her mouth. I could feel my penis growing against her tongue. Lacey started to massage my testicles and a sensitive area underneath my balls while moaning for my cock. She asked me if I had a condom. I replied, "Hell yes! Get it out and put it on for me." She put on the condom while sucking on my balls. I was ready to pound her and relieve the built-up tension. Lacey jumped back on my waistline, and as she slid down I put my dick inside of her sweet Irish cake. Lacey's sexually arousal was evident. I could feel her custard sauce dripping down my balls. By then I had her posted up on the wall, and I got to see why she had said in the beginning that she is a "fun-size."

As I am drilling her to the wall, Lacey is loud, and has her arms around my neck, scratching my back. I tossed her on top of the bed, and pinned her face down on the pillow with her ass in the air. I grabbed my dick by the base, and gently slid myself inside her. I said, "I'm going to go slow, so you can enjoy all of me." Then all of a sudden, I heard the sound of keys followed by someone entering the front door. I immediately stopped and said to Lacey, "Who the hell is here?" She said, "Don't worry, it's probably Thompson. He may just want to watch." I quickly gathered my things, and I apologized to Thompson on the spot. "I am sorry for intervening in your marriage, even though you left the gate open for me, and invited me into this for exploration. However, I'm not comfortable with you watching me screw your wife. Next, you may want to jump in, or turn on the situation and kill us both. Sorry, but I am not down with the reindeer games." Lacey and Thompson both giggled at me as I was leaving, and said there were no hard feelings. They wanted me to be comfortable with the situation because they had already discussed different possibilities.

I felt a bit naïve because they were setting me up for more than just an affair, also a lovers quarrel with a lot of moving parts. No Thanks, I'm going to stick to what I know. I am not going to pass judgment and say they are wrong or weird people. Some couples make arrangements to open up their relationship to add some spice. When doing so, does that mean that one of the individuals or both is not enough for the other? I have heard, and made excuses, even saying, "I'm too complicated for one person to understand and fulfill all sides of me." Well, that is why we have friends and family to meet that small social or emotional percentage that our partner may be lacking. When it comes to long-term connection, the mind needs to be conquered and endlessly nourished by each other.

People have different definitions of marriage, and the sanctity of marriage has been diminished and demolished by a new cultural norm. Marriage takes a lot of discipline and sacrifice. The sacrifice that is required is resisting temptation. The infidelity Lacey and I participated in occurred in our mind before the actual action. I do believe that Lacey did love and fall for me. She let me into her world of inner thoughts, and it taught me a valuable future lesson to guard my mind. To never let another person get a mental advantage over my partner. For the different sexes who read this book...do not be too concerned about protecting your bed and making sure that your companion is being true to the relationship. Protect each other's head because that is the sure pathway to the bed.

ACKNOWLEDGMENTS

First, I would like to thank my editor, Vanessa Gonzales. I came to you with this idea as a rookie writer, and you provided invaluable insight and coached me through the entire process—always available by phone or email to keep me on the right path. Thank you for your skills, professionalism, and honest feedback.

Alexis Gregory, my friend who allowed me to trick her into proofreading this project and providing honest feedback and additional perspective. Your talents extend beyond your normal day to day capacity. Thank you, Lex.

Special thanks to my sister, Kristina Hannon, who was happy to provide financial support to complete this project and believed in my goal.

Jason Anthony Crawford for photography, and Mir Shakur as the cover model image.

Last, but never least, my amazing wife, Shanae, for graciously giving her blessing to this project.

BOOK CLUB
QUESTIONS FOR DISCUSSION

Six Women 6 Flavors: From Your Head to Your Bed

The author opens the book with a quote by Isabel Allende, "For women, the best aphrodisiacs are words. The G-spot is in the ears. He who looks for it below there is wasting his time." Would you agree with that assessment?

Introduction Questions:

1. The author tells a story about his regretful experience with Amber because of his insensitive joke/comment. Can you recall a date when you said something your date found off putting, or the other person said something to you that made you check out on the person—maybe not by leaving immediately, but at least by no longer being open to letting that person into your heart or mind?
2. The author speaks about needing certain senses engaged for his body to react sexually. What are the mandatory senses that you need to have aroused for sex?
3. Is it more fun sharing unique sexual moments with someone you admire on a cerebral level?

Chapter I Questions

1. What is the curse that the author is referring to?

2. Is there something in your own life that you feel cursed about that is impacting you from forming a long-term relationship or sexual connection?
3. How many ways and times have you sabotaged a relationship on purpose?
4. The author talks about being influenced early on in his life to get the power, money, then pussy...in that order? What are the motives of this order? Do you have a secret order of operation to gain the upper hand in your own relationships?

Chapter II Questions

1. Have you ever dated a person just because people in your circle admire that individual?
2. Who introduced you to the sexual relationship "big leagues?"
   - How did you know you had arrived?
3. Do you mind a sexual partner who relies on your instructions to sexually please you? Would you prefer that your partner figure out your sexual preference on their own?
4. When the author speaks about his sex scene with Destiny in the new housing development out in the open, could you identify with a time when you were at risk of being caught doing something sexual in public?
5. Have you ever had to get sexual revenge like the author did with Destiny? Why and did it work?

Chapter III Questions

1. If applicable, how long did it take you to sleep with your best friend? Did you remain friends?
2. Is it possible to be best friends with the opposite sex and never cross the line sexually after 20 years of friendship? Do you believe that one of the party's secretly want a relationship?
3. The author provided 4 P's in order to have a successful relationship, would you trade any of them out, and if so, with what?

Chapter IV Questions

1. What about this chapter initially resonated with you as a reader?
2. Is it likely that people with sexual addictions have experienced sexual abuse?
3. What and when would you have change the relationship with Ashley if you were in the author's shoes?
   - Have you ever been in a similar situation?
4. What makes for a healthy sexual relationship in your opinion?

Chapter V

1. Thinking about when the author kissed Hanna so she would not forget his common name...have you ever done anything risky to make a lasting first impression?
2. Despite it resulting in the author's intent, do you view this sort of behavior as too aggressive or inappropriate?

3. The author believes that both parties in a relationship need to financially invest to demonstrate commitment. Do you agree?

4. The author made Hanna believe that he was okay with her dog being part of their relationship. Have you ever accepted a fear or uncomfortableness just to get closer to a person?

Chapter VI

1. The author felt that his niceness was his demise with Rachel. Why do nice guys finish last?

2. The author goes into depth about stereotyping. Did anything resonate with you in his comments and experiences regarding stereotyping?

3. Who is the best kisser you have experience and what made/makes them so good?

4. What type of man does Rachel need?

5. Describe perfect oral sex for you?

Chapter VII

1. What are your thoughts about dating sites? Have you had any experiences worth sharing?

2. Like the author, have you ever felt intimidated by the accomplishments of the person you were dating?
   - If so, how did you overcome that?

3. The author mentions that not being romantically aggressive in the beginning, diminished his chances with Sharmaine. What is a reasonable timeline to "round all the bases," assuming first base is kissing

and home plate is sexual intercourse?

Bonus Chapter

1. As a single person, what are your thoughts in getting involved with a married person who has an open marriage?

Final Questions

1. Which character do you think the author enjoyed writing about the most?
2. Which character do you think the author should have pursued until the end?
3. After reading this book do you value the intellectual connection more?
4. What was your favorite chapter or lesson? Why?

ABOUT THE AUTHOR

A.D. White grew up in Highland, California. He has a Master of Arts in Organizational Leadership from Azusa Pacific University. By day, he is a Contract Specialist for the U.S. Navy, and by night, a musician and writer. Penned under David White, he has two forthcoming, additional novels: *From Father to Daddy*, encouraging parents to be leaders in their homes, help children develop into champions, and restore broken relationships; as well as *Rushing to Fail*, a motivational book for young adults on transitioning to independence for the right reasons. He currently resides in San Diego, California with his wife, and is the father of four children. Learn more and follow his work at DavidWhiteAuthor.com.